Siân James was born and educated in West Wales, her family the usual mixture of teachers, preachers, poets and arsonists. Her literary style was formed in her early schooling in the war years when, due to paper shortages, any composition had to be completed in one page.

For thirty years she was married to Shakespearian actor, Emrys James, who got her writing, and admired all her sentences and the spaces in between.

She has had eleven novels published, including *A Small Country*, *Storm at Arberth* and *Second Chance*, all based in Wales, a collection of short stories, *Not Singing Exactly* and a memoir of childhood, *The Sky Over Wales*, and over the years has had five literary prizes.

She writes about love, compromise and forgiveness.

PARTHIAN BOOKS

Outside Paradise

Siân James

PARTHIAN BOOKS

Parthian Books
53 Colum Road
Cardiff
CF10 3EF
www.parthianbooks.co.uk

First published in 2001.
All rights reserved.
© Siân James
ISBN 1902638-19-0

Typeset by NW.

Printed and bound by Colourbooks, Dublin.

The publishers would like to thank the Arts Council of
Wales for support in the publication of this book.

With support from the Parthian Collective.

Cover: Girls with Kites by Jacqueline Alkema

A CIP catalogue record for this book is available from
the British Library.

Stories

Love, Lust, Life

Let's face it, we'd already talked about everything else, said everything there was to say. Childhood, parents, schools, holidays, babies, children, husbands, farming, teaching; we'd been over it all several times. I knew Glyn, her husband, devoted enough he seemed in a morose sort of way, her daughter Alison, her son Huw, their young families. She was on nodding terms with my husband Russell, who looks every inch the headmaster he is and my sister Gwenda, unmarried, who works in a solicitor's office and breeds Sealyhams.

You see, we'd been together for three months, off and on. Both of us dying of cancer, but Molly going for it with more panache, swearing more, cursing more, crying more; me altogether quieter, always the lady. (Even if you saw us both in the hospital's salmon-pink dressing gowns, waiting for our X-rays, you'd know at once which of us was the farmer's wife, which the teacher.) We were both reasonably attractive, now that our hair had grown back. Molly had a broad face and rather a wide nose, but the most beautiful lips and full breasts. I'm tall and thin with high cheek-bones and no figure to speak of.

Of course, as we're both in our fifties, talking about sex didn't come naturally to us. We'd often notice the pretty young nurses drawing together, looking naughty, having a giggle, but they were a different generation. Until that particular evening, we'd always skirted delicately round that most delicate subject. But now Molly had decided to plunge in.

'Sex,' she said, that evening, 'a strange business, isn't it? Very. There was never much of it in my marriage. Was it my fault, I wonder, or Glyn's? Of course we got married too soon, perhaps it's always too soon. I'd never been out with anyone else.

'Yes, I'd certainly fancied boys while I was at school, there was one boy in particular, oh, he was very handsome, and brilliant at games and a lovely singer as well, a nice light tenor, but of course he hardly knew of my existence.

'Glyn was older. He'd left the secondary school before I'd started there, but he started coming to the house with my brothers; he was a friend of my brothers. That's how I got to know him.

'I didn't know anyone else. We lived on a smallish farm a couple of miles outside the village, six miles from town, who was there for me to get to know? There was no one in the chapel we went to. Occasionally some traveller in animal feed would call and chat me up over a cup of tea in the kitchen, but it never came to anything. My father or my brothers would see to that. So I used to look forward to Glyn coming on a Saturday. Not that he came to see me. He had an old Morris van and he'd come to call for my brothers and they'd go to the pub for the evening, but when he brought them back he'd come in and stay for half an hour or so and I used to look forward to those times. He'd have a cup of coffee or some home-made wine and after a while he'd mellow and put his arm around me and I'd fling it away and he'd laugh and my brothers would laugh and that's how it would go on.

'Ours was a poor farm, since my mother's death, anyway. It was more comfortable while she was alive. She did a lot of cooking and cleaning and always kept a good fire in the grate. Not that it was anything like the Archers' farm at Ambridge even then, perhaps Welsh farms never are. Anyway it wasn't so bleak then – when she was alive, I mean. Spring was always a celebration, somehow. Not Easter or the religious festival – though she did go to chapel and believed in all that – but just the breaking of the earth's crust, lighter mornings, the first blossom on the blackthorn. There was always a renewal of hope then. My mother died of cancer. Well, it's a popular illness, isn't it? Yes, she'd be in her early fifties, too.

'Anyway, to get back to Glyn. Idris, the older of my brothers, told me that he was serious about me and wanted to take me home to meet his parents the next Sunday. "Get yourself a new dress," Idris said. And he gave me a ten pound note. Bloody hell, I knew it was serious, then. Ten pounds was a fortune in those days. I'd never even held a ten pound note before.

' "I don't really know him," I said. "I don't know whether I like him." "You can find out, can't you," Idris said. "Yes, but if I take this money, that'll be it, won't it?"

' "We like him. Dad likes him. He's a solid chap. They've got a really good farm, the Morrises, much bigger than ours, with a lot of modern outbuildings and modern machinery. You'd be a fool to let him go, there's plenty of girls who'd have him. And besides,

Alun is wanting to get married and it would be easier for him to bring Beatrice here if you went."

' "Beatrice Williams? I didn't know there was anything in that."

' "Yes," Idris said, "and a bit more than anything, too. Well, I know she's a bit older than him, but she's a big girl and she'd make something of this place. She'd have more interest, wouldn't she? You've never had the interest. That's natural. We don't blame you."

' "What about you, then? Aren't you going to get married?"

' "I wouldn't have to, would I? Not if Alun does. I'd be in charge of the farm, that would be enough for me. And if Beatrice has two or three little ones – to be absolutely honest there's one on the way now – that would be as many as we'd want, wouldn't it? As many as we've got room for. Anyway, that's the position. Have a think about it. No hurry mind. Only get that dress, in case you decide on it come Sunday."

'Beatrice Williams in the family way and our Alun the father. That's all I could think of that night in bed. But she was old, at least ten years older than Alun, about fifteen years older than me, well into her thirties.

'Idris and Alun were very close, always had been, and neither of them was close to me, but all the same, it was strange that I'd heard next to nothing about Alun and Beatrice. How long had they been courting? I couldn't imagine them making love. Where had they done it? He never brought her to our house.

Outside in the fields? Or in her widowed mother's bungalow after she'd gone to bed? I thought about them much more than I did about Glyn and me. I tried – and failed – to connect them with all the things I'd read in magazine stories, Mills and Boon and school books like *Wuthering Heights*. In a decent suit Alun, though a few inches on the short side, wouldn't be altogether deficient, particularly if he shaved off his sideburns, but Beatrice Williams had frizzy black hair and little round eyes like currants and she weighed about fifteen stone.

'I suppose you could say that I got married to make room for fifteen-stone Beatrice Williams. I deserved all I got, didn't I?

'Anyway, it could have been worse. Glyn's parents were decent enough and they liked me well enough, I think.

'After I'd been there to tea in my new dress and jacket – French navy, not too bridal – Glyn became my official sweetheart, and that winter started staying for the night every Saturday after being to the pub with Idris and Alun, unofficial that part, and we got married in early spring.

'Beatrice, married to Alun by this time, was already living with us, and I must say she was a startling worker and cheerful and affectionate too, making a big fuss of me on my wedding day and a big fuss of Alun every day. She was a good girl and there's no doubt that she pulled the farm together. And she certainly kept Alun happy.

'Glyn's parents expected me to work hard, but there you are, they worked equally hard themselves and they were very easy with money, fair play to them.

'I suppose the marriage turned out quite well on the whole, plenty of hard work, but I was used to hard work, and better conditions than I'd known before and more money for little luxuries. Glyn wasn't as silent and dour in those early days, before his father died leaving him all the responsibility. I had Alison the next year and Huw Meredydd the following one and then I went on the Pill. And after that we had a few years of illness and death, my father, Glyn's father, Glyn's mother; the black years, with even more work for me, nursing as well as everything else.

'And all this time, sex had been the least important thing. Just a strangely primitive rite that happened once a week or so, accompanied by a lot of grunting and sweating on Glyn's part and not much more than silent acceptance on mine. Once or twice when he bothered to kiss me first, or chatted and laughed with me, I got some hint of how it seemed to be in books, but nothing in me ever glowed or bloomed or sang, never mind exploded.'

Molly was silent for a while, lying back quite still on her pillows. Her face was rather flushed. For a moment I wondered about ringing for the nurse. When she next spoke her voice was quite different, low and tender, as it was when she was talking to her youngest grandchild.

'I'm going back twenty years now,' she said, 'back to the time I was about thirty-two or three. The children were at secondary school and we were comfortably off. Glyn was never as free with money as his parents had been, but I had a bed and breakfast business by this time, which was giving me financial independence – I'd even got myself a small car – as well as pleasure and a bit of company.

'Glyn never wanted to spend money on the house, but I'd soon got a bit saved and one year decided on having a second bathroom and the next year, to convert the attic into two small bedrooms for the children so that I could take over their bigger rooms for more visitors. I hated having to turn down bookings.'

Another silence, shorter this time.

'Well, this is it now. My spring awakening. Was it spring? Yes, early spring, February perhaps. Definitely before the Easter influx of B&Bs. His name was Mike Taylor. He was the builder who came to give us the estimate for the work I wanted doing. Glyn had met him in a pub in town, the landlord had put in a good word for him and Glyn had asked him to call the following week.

'He came early on the Monday morning. He was there by the front door when I got back from taking the children to the bus-stop in the village. "I'll get my husband," I said. "Come in and wait in the kitchen."

'Even in the first minutes I was aware of him, nervous of him, my mouth dry. He was about twenty-eight, tall, with very blue eyes in a thin, dark face. An arrogant face and an arrogant way of leaning against the porch and then following me silently into the house.

' "What the hell do you need me for?" Glyn asked, annoyed that I was expecting him to leave his work in the yard. "It's you that wants the bloody thing altered."

' "Yes, but he'll take more notice of you. He's that sort."

'So Glyn took his boots off and we went upstairs and Glyn

told him what we wanted done. "And I'll be getting another estimate," he said, "if I think you're charging too much."

' "Bloody farmers always think they're being overcharged," Mike said. "I'll give you my price and then you can tell me to fuck off. You'll enjoy that."

' "And don't swear in front of my wife," Glyn said.

'Mike glanced up at me with a sort of quiet insolence. "I'll get on with the measuring," he said.

'Glyn and I went downstairs. "I don't like him," I said. "I think I'll decide on old Sam Miles after all."

' "I'm not having that waster here. He's drunk oftener than he's sober. This chap will do the work in half the time."

' "I don't like him," I said again.

'Anyway, the estimate he sent us was reasonable enough and as he could start work the following week, I let Glyn ring up to accept it.

'I felt nervous again as I took him upstairs the next week. The attic had one small window. I remember looking out from it at the field where Glyn was ploughing and then back at him, where he was taking measurements for a Velux window we were having in the roof.

'And as though he could feel me looking at him, he turned to look at me. For a long time he looked; a long, silent appraisal.

' "Open your blouse," he said then.

' "What? What did you say?"

' "Open your blouse."

' "How dare you! Who do you think I am?" I felt myself

shake with anger.

'"You followed me up here. So let's see what you've got on offer. Open your blouse."

'It was such a shock that I burst out crying. You see, he was right. I had followed him up to the loft. He knew his way perfectly well, knew exactly what he had to do. Why had I gone up with him? Only because he was so full of . . . well, of something that I obviously wanted, I was shocked and ashamed how much. And now that I'd started, I couldn't seem to stop crying. It wasn't anger now, but shame and grief. And something else I could hardly name as it was such a new, such a new and overwhelming sensation.

'"Never mind, never mind," he was suddenly saying, his arms tightly around me. "I didn't mean it, I promise. Only I'm a direct sort of chap and I always think other people are the same. You see, I fancied you last week and I thought you fancied me. You did too, didn't you? You see, I could tell. But all right, you don't want to do anything about it. Well, it's up to you. It's your decision. Perhaps you've got used to a bit more style than I've got. You dry your eyes now and forget all about it. Right?"

'"Right." But he was still holding me very closely. Almost as though I was a child. But I wasn't a child, but a woman with a pain, a pain like hunger.

'"So you go downstairs and forget about this, all right?"

'"All right." Everything was all right as long as he went on holding me. By this time he'd opened my blouse and was stroking my breasts so tenderly and sweetly that I couldn't bear to break away from him. When I tried to move, it was like trying to move in a dream. I couldn't move.

' "Right. So now you go straight downstairs and forget all about this. OK? Oh, but what beautiful breasts you've got, what beautiful dark nipples. Can't I just kiss and so on for a minute or so before you go? Yes? Just say yes if you mean yes, because I don't want to upset you again. Yes?"

' "Yes."

' "Yes. Just for a minute or two, then. Oh, what a lovely body you've got. What a wonderful soft belly. What a beautiful curve. It's like the curve of the sky. Oh, and now I can feel the top of your sweet bush, such a . . ."

' "Stop it. Oh, stop it."

' "We can't stop now, can we? Can we? Do you think we can? You really want to stop? Listen, just kiss me then. We can kiss, can't we, before you go downstairs? Don't be afraid to kiss. Properly. That's right. Suck my tongue tight into your mouth. That's right. Oh, do it again. Again."

'Oh, it was shameless and wonderful, that kiss, which went on for ever, stirring every cell in my body to quivering, trembling life. How could I forget that kiss and what came after? I couldn't. Even if I was a Christian and hoped for eternal life, I couldn't renounce the memory of it or deny that it was the greatest, most wonderful experience of my life, because that was the time I came alive as a woman. That's when I came alive, crying and wet as a new-born baby, but a grown woman and a different woman.

'And every day afterwards, all the time he worked for us and later, I made love with him, had sex, committed adultery, sinned, sinned, with the same joyful and shattering abandon, relishing every new and extraordinary and undreamed-of thing we did together, he leading and pleading and petting and praising and me following, obeying, wanting everything. And then wanting it again.

'You'd think I'd have forgotten it now, wouldn't you. All that fever and passion. All so long ago. You'd think I'd want to forget it. All the intrigue and lies, the interrupted phone calls and the hurried, famished meetings. You'd think that after he left me, because of course he did, he did leave me, though not until he'd got married himself almost five years later and left the area. Still, you'd think I'd want to put it firmly behind me by this time. You'd think I'd want to spend my last weeks, or last days, thinking of higher things, wouldn't you? So many lovely things to remember. The rush of spring, the quiet of a summer evening, trees in autumn, trees, trees, mountains, snow on the mountains. All those lovely things. And babies. My own, Beatrice and Alun's little ones, my grandchildren, this new one, this new little life. But that . . . you know . . . that was the best of all. The best.

'Well, I wanted to say that, wanted to tell someone about it. My breasts and my thighs are aching just to think of it again. Love, lust, life. I don't know which it was.

'It'll be your turn tomorrow, Jane, won't it? And I bet you've had your moments, too, for all you look as though butter wouldn't melt. Your turn tomorrow.'

Molly died that night. So I didn't have to tell her, after all, of my sexual experiences. Anyway, they'd have been a dismal disappointment; one or two tentative pre-marital affairs and an uneventful, rather dull marriage.

I felt happy for Molly, though. And when Glyn and Alison and Huw Meredydd came to see me after the funeral, I was able to tell them: she had a good life. She told me she'd had a good life.

If I cried it was for myself.

Billy Mason From Gloucester

My mother had an Aunt Hester. Hetty. She was born back in the nineteenth century, had died before I was born, but of all my relatives, she's the one I'd like to have known. Hetty.

Her mother had died in childbirth and she was brought up, rather grudgingly it seems, by her grandmother. Life was hard for elderly widows in those days, and Hetty was allowed a small share in her grandmother's poverty. The cottage was small and sparsely furnished, food, mostly bread and potatoes, always in short supply and to make matters worse, she had no other children to play with; the nearest house being two miles away. She went to school in the nearest village, three miles away, until she was eleven, though her grandmother would keep her home whenever it suited her. In spite of her erratic attendance, she learnt to read and write; indeed when my mother was clearing out her house, forty years later, she came across three or four books she'd had as school prizes.

The headmaster's wife, a Mrs Matthews, had a large family and would often call her in to give her parcels of out-grown clothes and a slice of bread to eat on the long walk home, but, as she told my mother on one occasion, had never invited her in to play with her own children. I suppose no-one took much notice of her.

It was her love of wild animals and her ability to rescue and tame them which gave her life a purpose. It was considered a fairly easy task to rescue a fledgling magpie and keep it as a pet until the following spring when it flew away to find a mate, but even the headmaster was impressed when a blackbird accompanied her to school one year, waiting in a tree outside until the end of the day. 'Sir, Hetty's taught that blackbird to whistle Bobby Shaftoe,' one of the big boys announced. And Mr Matthews listened to their duet, Hetty inside the classroom, the blackbird outside, and afterwards patted her on the head. One spring, she rescued and reared a baby squirrel, a red squirrel, far more wild and shy than the grey, and even after she'd released it back into the woods, it would appear on a branch from time to time when she walked to school, as though still acknowledging a distant kinship. 'I've got a dratted flea in my bed,' her grandmother complained around this time. 'Oh, but I mustn't tell you or you'll be wanting it for a pet.'

In spite of her limited diet, Hetty grew very tall, so that when she had to leave school to nurse her grandmother who had developed sciatica and could do nothing for herself, she was able to get a morning job at Bryn Teg, the nearest farm, with Mrs Delia Evans who'd been given to understand that she was thirteen, and who was to prove a good friend.

Hetty's grandmother died when Hetty was fifteen and at that point Mrs Evans suggested that she should take a full time, living-in job at the farm. She was about to move there when her father turned up. He'd disappeared when his wife died, probably unwilling to contribute anything to his child's upkeep, escaping to

South Wales where he'd got a job in the mines and re-married. His second wife had eventually thrown him out because of his habitual heavy drinking and occasional violence, so that he'd returned to his native village and hearing of his mother-in-law's death, had gone along to her cottage, hoping for temporary accommodation.

He was astonished to discover his daughter there; he'd hardly given her a thought for fifteen years. (By this time he had another two daughters by his second wife, but was equally indifferent to them.)

Hetty listened to all his troubles, accepted his presence as she'd accepted every other of life's burdens, made up her grandmother's bed and prepared to look after him. He was by this time a sick man.

She cared for him for twenty years. He had the miner's disease, dust on the lungs, which prevented him from working, but not from drinking; he could manage to cajole money from her even when she had barely enough for food. My mother once asked her whether she'd been able to feel any affection for her father. 'No, only sorrow,' she'd answered tearfully. He died in 1914, just before the beginning of the first world war.

The war caused few changes in Hetty's life; she didn't miss any luxury food items because she'd never had any, and having no sweetheart or brother, wasn't as heartbroken as others about the young men who were being sent to France; she cared and worried about them, hated the idea of war, but wasn't personally involved.

She wasn't again invited to live-in at the farm; by this time Mrs Evans had five children so there wasn't even an attic available, so that she lived alone in her isolated cottage, becoming more and more of a recluse. She worked at the farm as the indoor maid-of-all-work, lighting the range at half past six every morning and scrubbing out the dairy and the flagstone floors of the kitchen and back-kitchen and the long passages, washing and mangling all the 'rough' - the bed linen, towels, overalls and aprons - cleaning vegetables, making bread, churning butter. Mrs Evans didn't ask her to work outside because she knew how upset she got at the way the farm animals were treated; she'd always send her home early when Emlyn Gelly arrived to kill the pig; she didn't even ask her to pluck a chicken or skin a rabbit. What she was able to do, she did with all her strength, but there were things she wasn't able to do and Mrs Evans accepted that. 'She's not like other people,' she'd say, 'and perhaps that's not such a bad thing.' She was aware that Hetty went round the rabbit snares that her husband laid out around his hedges, but never let on; she herself had often been sickened to see the poor mutilated creatures. 'Shoot them, by all means,' she used to tell her husband, 'I know what damage they do, but it can't be right to torture them.'

'I saw you out in Top Meadow earlier on,' she once said when Hetty had arrived a few minutes late for work. 'Was it mushrooms you were after?'

Hetty had blushed to the roots of her reddish hair, but had scorned to tell a lie. 'No, not mushrooms. Too early for mushrooms, Mrs Ifans. But when I find some I'll bring them up for your breakfast, be sure of that.'

'I know what you're doing, Hetty,' Delia Evans said after a

moment or two, 'and I don't blame you. Your heart is too soft, that's your trouble, but I won't say a word.'

What else did she find to do with her time after her long day at the farm? She occasionally went to evening service at Bethesda chapel on a Sunday when the weather was fine, but Mrs Evans told my mother that she wasn't a great one for God. 'I don't understand what He's doing, Mrs Ifans, letting all our young men face such danger. Ifor Stanley has been killed, they say, and his mother a widow with only him to help her with her bit of a smallholding. And even if those Germans lads are wicked as Mr Isaacs, Bethesda, seems to think, they've still got mothers haven't they?'

'It's not for us to reckon it out, Hetty. But thank goodness my boys are too young to go to the Front. They took Mat Brynhir, as it is, and two of our horses.'

It was in the spring of 1918, the morning of Palm Sunday, when Hetty found the injured man in the woods. She was picking primroses and violets to put on her grandmother's grave and they were so scarce that year that she'd had to go deep into Arwel woods before she'd got enough for a decent bunch. The man pulled himself up to a sitting position and stared at her. 'Don't split on me,' he said. Hetty didn't understand much English, but she understood the pleading in his eyes. She put down her flowers and took off her shawl and put it round his shoulders because he'd begun to shiver and sweat. 'I'm on the run,' he said. 'On the run from the army. They'll shoot me if they find me. Don't let them find me.'

'No,' Hetty said. 'No, no, no. I get you food.'

She looked hard at him. She had sometimes seen animals being driven to the slaughter house in town. It was Palm Sunday. She gathered up her flowers and walked quickly back to the cottage.

There was some soup on the hob. She heated it up, put some into a covered pot, placed it, with a piece of bread and a spoon, into a basket, put a blanket on top and walked back into the wood, walked hurriedly, fearing that the man might already be dead: she knew starvation when she saw it, knew the smell of death, too.

He hadn't moved; had either been too weak, or had perhaps trusted her. 'I'm a deserter,' he said - she didn't know that word - 'and they'll shoot me if they find me.'

'No,' she said. 'I say no.'

Then she started giving him spoonfuls of soup, very small amounts at first.

'Good,' he said.

'Cawl,' she said.

'Cawl,' he said.

She went on feeding him until his eyes closed. Then she took the shawl she'd lain on him earlier and folded it for a pillow, laid the blanket over him, and told him, as well as she could, that she'd be back when it was dark. She wondered whether he'd be still alive and wondered what she'd do with him if he was. How ever would she get him back to the cottage? He was certainly too weak to walk. Perhaps she'd have to leave him in the woods until he got stronger.

She still had some of her father's clothes which she'd washed and ironed but hadn't managed to give away because no tramps, these days, seemed to come so far out of their way as her cottage. She'd burn his army uniform and give him clean clothes and he could hide away in her grandmother's bedroom until the war was over.

After her dinner, the remains of the soup, she walked the three miles to Bethesda chapel to put the bunch of flowers on her grandmother's grave. She didn't intend to stay for evening service, but went into the chapel and for once managed to pray, tears falling down her cheeks as she did so. 'Let him live. Let him live.'

The Reverend Isaacs came in as she was coming out. 'Are you all right?' he asked.

'I'm all right. But what about the soldiers at the Front?'

'God cares for them, Hetty, every one.'

'No He doesn't,' Hetty snapped back at him. The Reverend Isaacs was to report that at her trial.

As soon as it was dark, Hetty set off to the woods with a basin of bread and milk in her basket. She shivered a little, remembering the story of little Red Riding Hood which Miss Jenkins had read to them in the Infants', but then smiled at her fear; she wasn't a pretty little child but a grown woman, nearly forty years old, her hair already grey and her back already stooped. And the poor soldier she was hurrying to see was weak as a sickly lamb.

He was still alive. She got him up to a sitting position and fed him the bread-and-milk.

'Good,' he said.

'Bara llath,' she said.

He looked worse than any tramp, he hadn't shaved for weeks, he stank of urine and faeces, but Hetty was ready to risk everything for him. He was a frightened man on the run and she had to hide him. She had no other thought.

He wasn't ready to try to walk, whimpering when she tried to get him to his feet, so reluctantly, she had to leave him where he was for another night.

The next morning she was up before dawn to take him some gruel before going to work. She found him a little stronger, got him on his feet, said he had to walk a short distance to a place where he'd be more adequately hidden. After walking a few steps, he collapsed onto the ground. 'My feet are on fire,' he said. 'No more walking.' She managed to untie the mud-clogged laces on his boots, though almost overpowered by the stench of his feet. After a few moments, she began to feed him the gruel, but this time he was able to take the spoon from her and feed himself.

She left him a bottle of tea and a piece of bread for his dinner and hurried to the farm.

'Hetty, you're not yourself this morning,' Mrs Evans said. 'Aren't you well?'

'Thinking about this war, that's all. When will it end, say? What does it say this week in Mr Ifans's paper?'

'Always telling us it's going to end, but nobody knows is my guess. And all our boys getting killed. Katie Williams, Hendre Fach, has lost three of her four sons and she won't last long, doesn't leave her bed, they say. Joe Morris's boy has been sent home but he'll never be right, his feet are like webbed feet, Joe says, something to do with being in those wet trenches for months at a time, and he may have to have one leg off because of the gangrene.... Great Heavens, girl, sit down for a minute. Put your head between your legs, you've gone white as milk. You'd never do as a nurse, would you?'

Hetty sat for a whole five minutes before she felt up to getting on with the butter making. And the whole time she was churning, the word gangrene, gangrene, gangrene was going round and round in her head.

That night she went off again with her pot of soup. 'Cawl,' he said, as she lifted the lid. 'Good cawl.' He ate heartily.

'Walk now,' she said when he had finished. She helped him to stand, hoisted his arms over one of her shoulders and half-carried, half dragged him along the dark path. Four times, when his groaning became too much for her, she had to let him rest for five or ten minutes. The journey, less than two miles by her reckoning, took almost four hours.

She let him lie on the doorstep while she went in to light a candle and re-kindle the fire. The kitchen had an earth floor with a rag rug in front of the hearth. She dragged the rug a yard or two into the room and brought down the quilt from her bed to lay on it; she knew he'd never manage the stairs that night. When she went out to help him in, he was already asleep. She had to wake him and force him, quite roughly, to take the last few steps. He lay down with a groan and was asleep again in less than a minute. Then she banked the fire, put a chamber-pot at his side and set out again for the wood to retrieve the blanket and the shawl.

It was well after midnight when she got to bed though she had, as usual, to be up at six. Her body ached with tiredness, but she couldn't sleep. She knew she could find him food, knew she could hide him away since no-one ever called on her, but what would happen if he had gangrene? At last she slept but dreamed about the war, about soldiers, Joe Morris's son amongst them, turning into large green frogs croaking in the slime of the trenches. The plague of Egypt, she was saying as she woke.

'You're looking even worse today,' Mrs Evans said. 'Sit down and have a basin of porridge before you start on the dairy. Can't have you fainting away again.'

'You're very kind to me, Mrs Ifans,' Hetty said. And burst into tears.

'Are you in trouble?' Mrs Evans asked her. But then realised she couldn't be; she was surely too old, had never even had a sweetheart as far as she knew, she was tall as a man, her chest was flat, her hair scraped back in a bun. 'Are you unwell? Are you having heavy bleeding, something like that? It's quite usual, you know, at your time of life.'

'No, it's nothing like that.'

Hetty sat over her porridge, still weeping, and Mrs Evans suddenly decided that what she needed was a bottle of tonic. 'I'll send you home early this afternoon, Hetty, so that you can go up to see Sal, Penpwll. She's got all the old herbal powders and mixtures that are better than anything Dr Forest prescribes and you save a guinea as well. Sixpence is all she charges. Spring is a hard time for man and beast and as you know I've got my sister and her family coming for Easter so I'll be depending on you at the week-end.'

Hetty was pleased to have a chance to visit old Sal, though she lived on the far side of the rhos. She told her how she'd lost her appetite, how tired she was all day and how she wasn't able to sleep at night. 'Please give me the strongest tonic you've got. It was Mrs Ifans, Bryn Teg, sent me. She says you're better by far than the doctor and cheaper, too.'

'She's right, gel fach. This is my special mixture, this green one. It's bitter, mind, but it purifies the blood like nothing else. You'll be strong as a stallion when you've got this down you. A teaspoonful twice a day in half a cup of water and that will be sixpence ha'penny with ha'penny back on the bottle.'

Hetty felt buoyant as she walked home, confident that the vile-looking green medicine would be the making of her soldier. And if one bottle didn't do the trick she'd get him another. And another.

That evening she managed to get his boots and socks off, and though his feet were sore and bleeding they didn't seem disfigured. He whimpered like a puppy as she put his feet into a bowl of warm, salt water, but seemed ready to do whatever he was asked. The next morning before she went to the farm she managed to get him upstairs and felt he was now safe. She washed him and gave him one of her father's old shirts to wear and helped him get into bed in the best room which had once been her grandmother's. The English she'd learned at school was coming back to her and she was beginning to understand most of what he said, though she still found it difficult to talk to him.

'I'm Hetty,' she said when she came home that evening. 'You?'

'Billy. Billy Mason.'

'Mam? Dad?'

He nodded his head. 'In Gloucester. You have parents? Mam, Dad?'

'Dead.'

'I'm sorry.'

'You write to Mam and Dad?'

'No,' he replied in an anguished voice. 'No. They mustn't know I'm alive. No-one must know.'

She picked up his uniform which was caked with mud and sweat. 'Llosgu,' she said. 'Burn.' She took every piece of his clothing out into the garden, built a bonfire and stood over it until nothing remained but clean white ash. She went upstairs again to try to tell him that he was no longer a soldier, but he was fast asleep. She breathed more easily.

'The tonic is doing you a lot of good, Hetty,' Mrs Evans said at the end of the week.

'Oh, it is.'

The next three weeks passed with relatively few problems. Billy, though unable to eat much, seemed a little stronger each day. He walked to the window of the bedroom and sat there for much of the time she was at work. Hetty was pleased that he didn't mention coming downstairs.

Occasionally he'd talk about the war. When he did, he'd

forget that she was there, talking fast and wildly so that she wasn't able to follow much of what he said. 'Jack. My pal, Jack. Went to look for him. Nothing left. Only one arm to bury. Everyone killed . Bodies everywhere. Trip over bodies. Parts of bodies even in the trenches.'

'Safe here now. Safe now.'

'I had home leave. Couldn't talk to my parents. Too frightened to go back to France. Got on the wrong train. Purposely. No-one looked at my pass. Swansea. Carmarthen. They'll shoot me when they find me. They'll find me. Soon. Soon.'

On those evenings when he became hysterical with fear, she'd put her arms round him and rock him to sleep.

It was midsummer when he started raving and shouting uncontrollably and Hetty realised that he had a high fever. She didn't know what to do with him, then. He'd take no food or water. Hetty didn't go to work, but all she could do was wet his lips and put a cold flannel on his forehead and tell him over and over again that he was safe.

One evening, when she hadn't turned up at the farm for three days, Mrs Evans tapped on her door. Hetty let her in and took her upstairs. 'He's dead,' she said in a very calm voice. 'I tried to look after him but he died. He was a soldier. I found him in Arwel woods. Billy Mason from Gloucester.'

She couldn't remember much of what happened after that. Mrs Evans was very kind and stayed with her while all the others came and went; Mr Evans, the doctor, the policeman, the army officer, the undertaker. 'I promised they wouldn't find him, but he's safe from them now,' she said over and over again. While Mrs Evans spent her time telling them all that Hetty was different from other people, too soft-hearted, but a good woman for all that.

They didn't listen to her. She was put on trial for harbouring a deserted soldier and was throughout, the subject of great ribaldry. 'That's one way of catching a man,' 'Aye. She burnt all his clothes and wouldn't let him out of bed for three months.' 'An old maid's revenge. I reckon he'd have been better off in France.' 'Aye, it did for him in the end.'

She was found guilty and sentenced to eighteen months hard labour, but was released a month after the armistice.

During her trial, which had been widely reported, her two half-sisters from South Wales - one of them, my grandmother - contacted her, visited her in Swansea Jail and remained in touch with her ever afterwards. 'Two sisters I never knew I had,' she told Mrs Evans. 'And so kind, you wouldn't believe.'

In the spring of 1919, she was considered strong enough to go back to work at the farm.

Later that year, Billy Mason's parents sent her a letter of thanks and a framed photograph of their son, taken when he had first joined up. He looked so young and unmarked by war, that she didn't recognise him. All the same, she kept it on the dresser for the rest of her life.

I have in now on my mantelpiece. 'Billy Mason from Gloucester,' I tell friends. 'No, not a relative. Just a soldier my Great-Aunt Hester picked up in the woods.'

Not Singing Exactly

I was brought up quite strict, to know right from wrong, to be careful of what you were at and it's stayed with me up to a point. Not that there was all that love involved in it, it was more fear really. Three girls and one boy and my dad left home when I was five and then we had a stepfather before I was seven. My stepfather was the strict one, well perhaps he had to be with four kids around and not his own. My mum had a good job, supervisor in a dress factory and he was some sort of traveller, so there was a fair bit of money, I suppose, and that means you can afford to be decent, paying your bills and so on. My two sisters were older than me and when they left school they got a job together in the Majestic up town and lived in, so there was only my brother and me left at home, he was the youngest of the family, my brother Terry, three years younger than me.

When I was fifteen and longing to be shot of school, I used to skive off home for the afternoon sometimes and just sit around having cups of tea on the new settee with the telly on and the gas fire and dreaming about being married to a really rich man and not have to work for a living, no factory, no shop, not even part-time up the market. One day my mum came home and I told her I'd got a headache and she said she had a headache too, and we sat together drinking tea and she offered me a fag and I said no because of cancer and she said how I was the most sensible of all her kids and she had this fit of crying. And then she told me she hadn't got a headache only she had just had an abortion, but I wasn't to tell Dave – that was my stepfather – or he'd kill her because he was always on about having a kiddie of his own. She cried for about an hour and I didn't know what to do except make her more and more cups of tea. I hadn't realized before that she was frightened of him too, Dave I mean. He could be a devil. I don't think he ever beat her up, not as far as I know, but he used to lay into my brother for any little thing, coming in late, spilling his food, losing his anorak, anything, and it used to turn her stomach, she'd cry and pull at his arm and beg him to stop, please, but he wouldn't. We all hated him, her as well. I only realized it that day.

Anyway that was the day I knew I had to leave home and it was that night I started seeing this boy Rob. Well, I'd had a bit of a chat and a laugh with him before, but that night I went up the park with him, which was the first time for me, and in about six months I got married to him.

It was three weeks after my sixteenth birthday, the wedding, a really lovely summer day. There were two bunches of white roses in the register office so it seemed a bit like a church, a nicer place altogether than I'd expected, quite posh really. My mum and one of my sisters came and my mum treated us to a meal in the Gatehouse after, chicken salad and jacket potatoes and white wine. She'd never even tried to persuade me not to get married, she knew I was pregnant and that there was no way I could live with her and my step-dad after, him being so strict.

'It's a pity you're starting on a family so young,' she said, 'but there you are, you're more sensible than I was and perhaps you'll be careful after this one.' 'For God's sake go to the Women's Clinic in Broad Street,' my sister Rose said, 'they look after you there. If only you'd said something to me two or three months ago you could have got rid of this one.' 'I didn't want to,' I said, because you have to say that, not liking to admit how frightened and stupid you were.

'Well, it's nice they've got a bit of a flat and they can be together and we'll be able to help them a bit, won't we,' my mum said, and I could see how she was pressing Rose's leg under the table and then Rose said yes they'd do their best and gave me a fiver and a fiver from Tina my other sister who hadn't been able to come because she was on lunches.

Rob and me went to Priory Gardens after and I cried a bit because of leaving home which was a nice place except for Dave and because the bit of a flat we had was really only one room, a long damp room without even a lampshade or a proper cooker, with the bathroom two floors up.

'Tell you what, girl, let's grab a hitch to the country,' Rob said. He's that sort of a person, ever so rough, like all his family, but really nice when you need it most. I could never understand why he wanted to marry me, he was twenty-three and there was some really attractive girls I'd see him hanging around with and I was small and mousey with no figure to speak of, though I've got a bit more now.

Anyway it really cheered me up, the thought of going to

the country on such a beautiful day. When Dave – my step-father – first came to live with us, he used to take us out every Sunday afternoon for picnics or for ice-creams, usually to the country somewhere, once to Stratford-upon-Avon which was only an hour away but seemed like another world. He used to make a fuss of Terry in those days, he was quite his favourite in those days.

We walked to the roundabout at Highcross and then got a hitch almost at once from a lorry driver and when Rob said we were going on a one-day honeymoon he said he knew just the place and he took us off the motorway to this village and dropped us where there was a sign saying to the river and that's where we went. And we lay down by the side of this wide, slow-moving river and looking up we could see patterns of leaves against a blue, blue sky and there wasn't any cows or mosquitoes or even people. It was like paradise really, and I kept dozing off because of the wine I'd had and I could feel the baby lurching about a bit in my stomach but it was a lovely feeling that day.

We stopped there till about six or seven and then we walked to the pub and we had some beer and crisps and Rob said did they do bed-and-breakfast and the barman said yes and we stayed there the night. I'd never stayed anywhere before except two weekends in Brownie camp, so of course I often think of that country pub, the little clean bedroom with pink wallpaper and the lovely crisp sheets on the bed, but most of all I remember the afternoon lying by that quiet river.

The place we had wasn't too bad at first. I had a job cleaning a couple of floors of this office block which was quite easy except for leaving a nice warm bed at six every morning. Rob used to say he was in furniture restoration, stripping chairs and that which they bought at auction and tried to sell to shops after, but I always knew that whenever he had a thick wad of dosh it hadn't come from that. It used to frighten me because as I said I wasn't used to that sort of a life and I was always nervous of the police coming. Of course I didn't tell my mum.

To tell you the truth I didn't see my mum very often now. Dave didn't want me calling on them. Even though I was married he was always saying I was a tart and that I'd let them down. 'It was all your mother's fault,' he used to say, 'she'd never let me give you a good hiding.' He gave us plenty of good hidings when we were small, he'd once taken the strap to Rose when she was fourteen, pulled her knickers down and laid her over the bed, but my mum had screamed at him that she'd take us all away if he as much as touched any of us again and though he'd pretended to laugh, oh big threat, he never did except for poor Terry. And also I wasn't very keen on my mum coming to see me because of the room being so crowded and untidy specially after Mandy was born. And then I got pregnant again almost immediately and we thought it would be nice to have two close together and after that I'd go to the clinic and ask them to put me on the Pill, but the next one turned out to be twins, two more girls, Tricia and Debbie, so I had three in just over fifteen months and before the end of the year, Rob was in prison for theft, stealing cars and breaking and entering, two years, and there was I, just eighteen and trapped for ever in this long damp room, my only glimmer of hope that Dave would drop down dead with a heart attack so that I could move back home. He's fifty if he's a day and he's always on about the hard life he had in the army and how hard he works now, so why can't he drop down dead like other men seem to, but no, I never get any luck.

So of course I have to live by shoplifting because my giro doesn't stretch even to the bare necessities and I've learnt that it's no use asking for the things you need because they only send you from one office to another at the opposite end of town, very easy with twins in the pushchair and the other not able to walk more than a few yards so that a simple bus journey is a nightmare and by the time you get there the office is closed or they give you all these forms to fill up and tell you to come back next week. They won't even give you an electric kettle when yours is broke. 'You don't have to use Pampers,' this woman said to me once. I'd like to see her washing nappies for three babies with no hot water on tap and nowhere to dry them, I really would. There's not even enough to buy food with, let alone the train fare to see Rob once a month. I don't smoke and I never go out in the evenings but I do get a bottle of sherry once a week, the cheapest they have, and a paper to see what's on the telly and nobody can live on less.

I'm not so nervous as I used to be. I've thought about it and I know it's the only way I can live and that makes it easier. I hardly ever take anything from the supermarkets because they've got all these cameras and security, but the little shops, I tell myself, wouldn't be so likely to take me to court because they're all doing badly and I reckon it could make them a bit more sympathetic, though I could be wrong. There's a small bread shop up our way and it has one middle-aged woman serving and another clearing up and I always get my bread there round about half nine in the morning when it's empty, and when it's being sliced I nearly always manage to take a packet of sandwiches, egg or cheese, from the top of the counter and slip it into this bag I have on the back of the push-chair. You have to be careful of mirrors, but so far it's always been all right in that shop. Greengrocers are quite easy, you can almost always pick something up from the display by the door or outside, you can usually pick up a cauliflower though it's not a vegetable that any of us likes, a couple of bananas are much more useful, mashed banana is a good tea for the little ones.

It's ever so easy to pick up clothes from a charity shop because the women who serve there are only there for a natter and couldn't care less. It's not very nice to steal from charity, but I can't afford to be choosy and I think the people who give the stuff wouldn't mind our having it and I never take more than I need and it's usually only babygros and little sweaters. Rose and Tina, my two sisters, give me plenty of cast-offs, though they're not my style, being tight and rather tarty, but they certainly make Rob's day when I visit him. I'm fatter than I was and he likes it. Myself, I like something a bit more plain.

Anyway, I had to have some winter boots. Autumn had been a trial, months of pouring rain, and I only had trainers. My feet are long and very narrow and nothing Rose and Tina gives me is any good and I looked in all the charity shops as well, so I knew I had to go to the DSS again to beg and fill in forms and go from one place to another like I said before. Luckily, Terry my young brother has just left school and he said he'd come over to look after the kids for me this one afternoon so I could go by myself without the hassle of getting the push-chair on the bus and so on. The twins sleep most of the afternoon and Terry is quite good with Mandy, tosses her up in the air and turns the music on really loud to make her laugh. He wants to come to live with us, but I'm sure he'd only regret it with no space and washing everywhere. Kill Dave instead, I tell him, but of course, only in fun.

Well, I was walking past some of those smart shops in Cavendish Road to get to the 66 bus stop when a woman comes out of one of the antique shops and nearly knocks me over. 'Excuse *me*,' she says, but the way she says it you know that what she means is, get out of my way you shabby lower-class person, and I've never got the quickness of mind to answer back. One thing about Rob is he's never, ever lost for words. Anyone who's even half rude to him gets it back with knobs on. But me, I only burn inside. That woman makes me feel a hundred times worse than I already was. She's got one of these huge wrap-over coats on, made of so much lovely material, cashmere or something, that would keep a whole family warm and the most gorgeous soft leather boots that you'd never feel the cold again in and I feel a rush of hatred for her and all her sort. The strange thing is that when she disappears from sight, I march straight into the shop she's just come out of – not the sort of place I'd ever go into in a normal frame of mind – quite determined to nick something from there. To get even with her, I suppose, though I admit it doesn't make any sense.

'May I help you?' a saleswoman says. She has silver hair

and pointy tits and a face which looks too smooth to be real.

'I'm looking for a present,' I hear myself saying, 'a birthday present for my mother. Something a bit unusual but not too expensive.'

She comes out from behind the counter. I'm surprised that she seems to be taking me seriously. 'What sort of price did you have in mind?' she asks me in quite a pleasant way, not the sort of half-choked voice I'd expected. 'We haven't much under twenty pounds but what we have is very good quality and of course quite exclusive.'

'I was hoping for something about fifteen pounds,' I say, 'perhaps a little brooch in the shape of a fan.' Fifteen pounds, that's a laugh, I couldn't manage fifteen pence on top of the bus fares.

She's getting quite anxious to find something for me, but everything is in cases and glass cupboards so I can't see anything I can lift, though I keep looking around. I must look as restless as a bird in a cage.

'This is pretty and only twelve pounds fifty,' she says and brings out a brooch, a little poodle with a shiny collar. I laugh a bit hysterically because it's such a daft-looking thing. 'Oh it's nice,' I tell her, 'but I don't think it would suit my mother.'

'I see.' She walks off to another stand without closing the case she got the poodle out of and I grab the first thing I can, which is a silver bracelet, and shove it in my pocket. 'I think perhaps I'll leave it for today,' I tell her and walk quite slow to the door, but before I get to it there's a man standing there. I hadn't even seen him at the other side of the shop, but he's seen me all right.

'Could you follow me to the office please,' he says. I make a grab for the brass door handle, but the door doesn't budge. 'Could you follow me to the office please,' he says again in a very gentle sad voice and the woman with silver hair is also looking sad and I don't know what to do but follow him, so I do.

And we get there in spite of my legs feeling like tree trunks instead of legs and he shuts the door and locks it. 'I'm afraid I shall have to phone the police,' he says in the same voice. 'Would you like to put the bracelet on my desk?' It doesn't seem worth telling him about the three kids and Rob in prison and not having boots. I think about it but I decide not to, if I'd been caught with a loaf or a tin of mince it would be different. I don't say anything, just take the bracelet out of my pocket and put it on the desk like he said. We both look at it.

Then I look at him. He's in between middle-aged and quite old, the sort of man who looks exactly like any other man in a dark suit, short faded hair and a face like a kid's drawing of a man, straight nose and a line for a mouth. He's looking at me quite blankly without any anger, just blankly. Looking and looking.

'Pull your skirt up,' he says then, his voice shaking a bit.

I take it that he's making a deal with me and I don't even think of refusing it.

I ease it up as far as it will go. It's a very tight skirt I got from Rose, the sort of thin black material that gets very creased. I have these white cotton knickers on, the sort you wear to go to the clinic. He looks at me for a long time and I look at a spot on the wall just beyond his head. I wonder if this if what he had in mind all along.

'Turn round,' he says after what might have been two or three minutes but feels like thirty. I turn round. I wonder if the woman with silver hair is his wife.

'Can I go now?' I ask after an even longer time.

'Yes. Go now.' His voice is even more shaky.

I tug my skirt down, trying to press out the creases. He's not looking at me. He unlocks the door, opens it and then stands to one side to let me pass.

As I go I pick up the bracelet again and put it on my arm. I didn't think he'd stop me and he doesn't.

The woman at the counter is busy with something and doesn't raise her head as I pass her.

This time the door opens as soon as I pull it.

All the way down Cavendish Road and Market Street I think about the afternoon when Rob and me got married, sitting high up in the cab with the lorry driver, Rob with his arm around me, blowing smoke in my hair and saying rude things to make me laugh. And about lying on the grass by the river, watching the pattern of leaves against the sky and listening to some birds, not singing exactly but making little happy noises.

Then I start to think about where I can sell the bracelet and whether I'll get enough for a pair of boots.

Strawberry Cream

I was eleven that summer, but according to my mother, already moody as a teenager, 'What can I do?' my constant cry. 'I'm bored. What can I do?'

'There's plenty to do. What about dusting the front room for me? Your grandmother and your Auntie Alice are coming to tea on Sunday.'

I hated our front room which was cold and shabby, the furniture old-fashioned, the ceiling flaking and pock-marked with damp and the once mauve and silver wallpaper faded to a sour grey and wrinkled at the corners. Our whole house was depressing, each room having its own distinctive and unpleasant smell, the front room smelling of mushrooms, the living room of yesterday's meat and gravy and the back kitchen of Oxydol and wet washing. 'Dusting doesn't alter anything,' I said.

I expected my mother to argue with me, but she seemed too dispirited. 'I know it doesn't,' she said. And then, 'Just get yourself a nice library book and pretend you live in a palace.'

Was that what she did? She was always reading; two and sixpenny paper-back romances with fair-haired girls standing on windy hills on the covers, their skirts gusting out prettily around them, their long tresses streaming behind, but their make-up immaculate.

Once I'd tried reading one of them. *Caterina breathed in as Milly tugged at the corset strings around her waist. 'Tighter,' she commanded sharply.*

'Yes, Miss Caterina,' Milly murmured in a humble voice. She loved her mistress with a blind adoration and wanted nothing but to serve her.

I continued the story in my own way. *Milly squeezed the juice of the deadly nightshade into her mistress's drinking chocolate and chuckled as she imagined pulling the strings of the shroud tighter and tighter around the tiny waist.*

I was fiercely egalitarian. My Dad was a farm labourer and he had the same attitude, speaking to his boss with unconcealed disdain. 'You want me to do … what?' 'Don't you think that would work?' his boss would ask. 'Of course it wouldn't bloody work, but I'll do whatever you tell me. It's all one to me.'

My mother served in the village shop for two pounds ten a week and she was pretty cool too. I don't think she ever demanded a decent wage, just helped herself to groceries to make up the deficiency, mostly items that fitted neatly into her overall pockets. We were never short of packets of jelly, corn-flour, mixed herbs, caraway seeds. Or bars of chocolate. That summer, Cadbury's Strawberry Cream was my passion and she brought me one every single lunch time. And every afternoon I'd snap the bar into eight squares, sniff every one, bite a hole in the corner and very slowly suck out the oozy pink cream, afterwards letting the sweet chocolate casing melt on my tongue. Sometimes I could make it last a blissful half hour.

My father's boss, Henry Groves, had a daughter called Amanda who was three or four years older than me and went to a boarding school in Malvern. I'm sure she wouldn't have chosen to spend any time with me had there been any older and more sophisticated girls in the village, but there weren't; she'd knock on out front door and stand there silently until I condescended to go out with her.

We usually walked along by the river, kicking at stones and muttering to one another. 'What's your school like?' 'Deadly. What about yours?' 'Deadly.' We had nothing to talk about.

We could never think of anything to do either. What was there to do? The sun beat down on us mercilessly every afternoon, the hours stretched out long and stagnant as sermons; I felt dusty and dried-up as the yellowing grass on the verge of the path.

'Don't you have any adventures at your school?' I asked her one day. 'Don't you have midnight feasts and so on? Pillow-fights in the dorm?' I wanted some sort of conversation; lies would be fine by me. Her eyes narrowed. 'What rubbish have you been reading? How old are you anyway?'

'Thirteen.' She looked across at me. I was tall and sturdy for eleven. She was small and, I suppose, rather pretty; a turned-up nose and so on, floppy hair and so on. My God, she looked a bit like the lovesick girls on the covers of my mother's Mills and Boon. Why was I wasting my summer afternoons with her?

'Well act your age then. Pillow-fights ! For God's sake!'

I tried again. 'Do you have a boy-friend?' I asked.

She gave me a friendlier look. 'That would be telling.' I

was definitely on the right track.

'I'll tell you if you tell me,' I said, trying to recall conversations I'd overheard on the school bus; a fierce, fat girl called Natalie Fisher, who was about fifteen I suppose, but looked thirty, who was always whispering loudly about 'doing it.' I could pretend I was 'doing it' with Joe Blackwell who sometimes helped me with my Science homework.

'You go first,' she said.

'I've got this boy-friend called Joe Blackwell.'

'And?'

'He's tall and he's got red hair and millions of freckles. Quite attractive.'

'And?'

'And ... and we 'do it' sometimes.'

She was suddenly looking at me with alarming admiration; her eyes dilated and her lips moist. 'Go on,' she said.

'Nothing much more to say. Your turn now.'

'Let's cross the river. It's more private in the woods. We can talk better over the other side.'

We hadn't seen a soul all afternoon, but if she wanted to cross the river I was quite prepared to wade across with her. It made a change.

We took off our sandals and splashed across. The sky was white and glaring, the stones in the riverbed were hot and sharp.

'These are my father's woods,' she said.

There was no answer to that. I knew as well as she did whose bloody woods they were. 'This is where Joe Blackwell and I

... you know.' I said. It seemed a way to get even with her.

'Show me what you do,' she said, moistening her lips again with the tip of her small pink tongue. 'Show me how you do it.' She sat on the ground and pulled me down with her.

'I can't do it with a girl,' I said, my voice gritty with embarrassment.

'Yes you can, of course you can. Don't you think I know anything.' She was opening her dress and pulling me to her. ' Do you like my breasts?' she asked, tilting them up towards me.

I hated breasts. My Auntie Alice was always getting hers out to feed her baby, great mottled things, large as swedes, but more wobbly; I hated having to see them, the shiny mauve veins; the pale, wet, puckered nipples.

Amanda's breasts were different, small and delicate, creamy as honeysuckle, pink-tipped. She snatched at my hand and placed it over one of them. It seemed like some small, warm animal under the curve of my palm. 'What now?' she asked. 'What do we do next?' Her voice was creaky like the hinge of a gate.

Her nipple hardened under my touch. I felt shivers go down my body like vibrations in the telegraph wires. I closed my eyes as my fingers circled over and over her breasts. 'We have to do this part properly first,' I said.

I peeped at her face. Her eyes were closed. She looked like the picture of Saint Winifred in church; as though she was seeing angels.

'Now what?' she asked again. I lowered myself onto my elbow and licked her nipples, one after the other. Her eyes flicked open in surprise. 'Licking?' she asked. 'Licking,' I said firmly. 'Don't you like it?' 'I think so. Do you?'

The shivering started up again, it was lower now, my belly seemed to be fluttery as a nest of fledglings. 'Yes, I like it.' I tried to sound non-committal, but suddenly I was lifting her towards me and sucking, sucking her little round breasts.

'That's all I know,' I confessed at last. Other images which were beginning to besiege my mind seemed altogether too bizarre. 'I don't know the rest of it,' I repeated.

I thought she'd be annoyed, expected her to fasten up her dress and flounce off. She wasn't, though, and didn't. 'Well, we can do this part again, can't we?'

And we did. We did it again and again all through the last dog days of that summer. Every fine afternoon we'd set off wordlessly along the same path, crossing the river at the same spot, lying down under the same trees, finding the same stirrings of pleasure.

At the beginning of September, it got damp and cold, the leaves lost their lustre, the birds grew silent, the woods began to smell of rust and wet earth and we realised that our time was running out.

'I'm going back to school next week,' Amanda said one Friday afternoon, 'so I suppose we'd better say good-bye.'

I raised my mouth from her breast and sat up. 'Good-bye,' I said. I felt something almost like sadness, but wasn't going to let her know.

'Perhaps we'll do the other part next year,' she said.

'Perhaps.'

I never saw her again. Before the Christmas holidays my father had found a better job and we'd moved from our horrid old house to another that wasn't quite as horrid, and my mother worked in an office instead of a village shop.

I went to a different school and forgot Joe Blackwell. But I never quite forgot those afternoons with Amanda: my strawberry cream summer.

John Hedward

'Julia and Claire have each other,' the members of Appleyard told one another, 'they're very close and they were never close to Ben. After all he was only four.'

'Ben was a loner,' Deirdre Macabe said. 'He was the same age as Patsy, but he never played with her. He certainly didn't like girls.'

They all thought about Ben who was dead; dark, stocky, unsmiling.

'He had this imaginary friend,' Eric Smith said then. 'He didn't need anybody else.'

Eric seemed more reconciled to the little boy's death than the rest of them. Yet he had been fondest of him. The only one with no children of his own, he had lavished time and attention on Ben.

'John Hedward,' Eric continued, taking his pipe out of his mouth again. 'That's what he called him, his little mate. Hedward. Most particular about the 'h'. Quite a lad. Red-haired. Could climb any tree in the world. Frightened of the dark, though. And thunderstorms. When the inspector asked us why Ben had gone all that way on his own, I nearly told him about John Hedward.'

'I'm glad you didn't,' Tim Austin said, rather shortly. He worried about Eric. He wasn't quite one of them. Older for one thing. The only one of working-class origins. Not that that made any difference of course.

'The thing is,' Sheila Armstrong said in her quietly forceful way, 'the thing is, Ben is dead. We've just got to accept it. We can't do anything for Ben. All we can do now is to take special care of Julia and Claire. After all, poor Barbara is beyond anything.'

They all sighed their agreement. Poor Barbara was definitely beyond anything. The children's father had come down from London for the funeral, but his presence had been no help. The little girls hardly remembered him and Barbara had thanked him for coming as though he were a complete stranger, seeming openly relieved when he went. She'd gone back then to her large dark canvases, standing in front of them as though they held all the answers, refusing to talk. She was certainly beyond taking any notice of her daughters.

Not that she had ever taken much notice of any of her children, Deirdre thought, conscious and a little ashamed of her disloyalty.

Deirdre knew that she was different from the others at Appleyard and it troubled her. They gloried in all the tough outdoor work – they lived on their market garden – as much as their painting, sculpture and pottery. They made their own bread, wine, butter, cheese. The children too had their own tasks and were expected to create their own pleasures. They believed that a conscious determination on simplicity would result in harmony and serenity.

But Deirdre often longed for a small centrally-heated

house near some shops and a nice park, Patrick coming home from his office at six o'clock, the girls in their dressing-gowns, and fish fingers for tea. Less creative than the others, she found herself with most of the household chores. How easy it would be to clean a small semi-detached house, hoover its bright carpets. The vast Appleyard rooms with their flagstone floors and draughts were beginning to get her down.

She caught her husband looking at her and tried to smile. She must strive to be like the others, she knew that. Like poor Barbara, for instance, who was really the most dedicated of them all, certainly the most gifted. They could surely bear her temporary withdrawal, Deirdre told herself, without feeling bitter about it.

As soon as the meeting was over, she went straight up to see Julia and Claire. 'Good night, little ones,' she said, giving them each a hug and a kiss. They were surprised, but not unduly discomfited. Deirdre was accepted as rather wet, but her soda scones made up for it.

With so many substitute parents anxious about them, Julia and Claire hardly noticed their mother's neglect.

In school, too, everyone was especially kind to them, friends – and even enemies – bringing them sweets and comics, and their class teacher inviting them home to tea.

On the day of the funeral, the headmistress had called them in to her room to give them one of her little talks.

'At the moment, you would probably like to forget all about your dear little brother,' the headmistress had said, 'his sweet ways, because remembering him is inseparable from the pain of losing him. But I'm going to ask you to make every effort to remember him, to make friends with the pain, so that his memory will remain with you to enrich the precious fabric of your childhood. Now, will you promise me to try?'

Both little girls had nodded their heads vigorously, Claire's fractional delay being only to make sure of Julia's reaction. 'Poor, brave little girls,' the headmistress had said.

And then in her normal brisk voice, 'And now you can spend the rest of the morning sorting out the P.E. equipment for me. You'd like that, wouldn't you?' They'd nodded their heads again, even more vigorously.

And ever afterwards to Claire, who was only just seven, the memory of Ben's death, which was to enrich the precious fabric of her childhood, was irretrievably mingled with the dusty smell of the plimsolls, bean bags, ropes and team bands which she and Julia had so carefully and tidily arranged in their different cardboard boxes on that morning after his funeral.

Only in bed at night did they ever talk about their dead brother. They worried, then, because they didn't miss him as much as they felt they should. Claire, in particular, felt very guilty, she knew she'd been far more upset when Donald, the old sheep-dog, had died.

'Anyway, I cried at the funeral,' she told Julia one hot August evening when she couldn't sleep.

'No you didn't. You just sniffed. I was watching you. Patsy cried all the time without even trying. Her face was all red and blotchy.'

'That was because she wasn't allowed to go to the funeral. She thought there was going to be balloons like we had for the Fête. That's why Patsy cried.'

'Ben didn't like us, that was the trouble,' Julia burst out. 'He didn't like us a bit.'

'He didn't really like anyone except John Hedward.' Claire sighed deeply. 'Julia, I want to ask you something.'

'He liked Eric,' Julia said, 'because he let him have matches.'

'And use the hatchet. Deirdre spoke to him about that over and over, I heard her. But Eric never took any notice. That's why he liked Eric. Because he never refused him anything. Mummy said he wasn't to have a pocket-knife, even Marcus hasn't got a pocket-knife and he's nearly six.'

'If only he'd liked us just a bit. Patsy can't wait for us to come home from school. Deirdre says she's at the gate half an hour early sometimes.'

'Patsy lets me bath her,' Claire said, 'and read to her at bedtime. She thinks I'm a very good reader.'

'Well you're not.'

'Patsy thinks I am. I read and read to her. Whole books. Ben never wanted me to read to him.'

'He used to shout if I went near him.'

'I went to his room once when he was having a nasty dream and he just said, "Go away, Nit".'

'He used to call me Fatface. Once he called me Bum.' It

pained Julia to remember.

Claire wrapped a piece of blanket round and round the fingers of her left hand. There was something she longed to ask Julia, but somehow didn't dare. She sighed hugely again.

Julia settled herself to sleep, but Claire still felt hot and restless. After counting to a hundred very slowly and reciting the three-times-table until she got stuck, she wondered if a prayer would help her. Mrs Bowles, the headmistress, and Miss Denman seemed sure that prayer helped everyone, but at Appleyard no one seemed convinced. Deirdre said it helped those it helped, Eric thought it was whistling in the dark, the others seemed upset about the subject. Like Miss Denman was when she had told her about Belinda being on heat and rolling about and calling for a mate. 'It's not a suitable item for your news book,' Miss Denman had said. You could never be sure what grown-ups would get fussed about. Life was very strange and very difficult. And it seemed to be getting worse. Ben's death, even though she couldn't pretend that she really and truly missed him, as she'd missed Donald, had certainly made her very uneasy.

'I feel outside myself,' she had told Julia the previous evening. 'I've never been outside myself before. And sometimes I don't seem to remember who I am inside. I mean, who I'm outside of.'

'Don't be silly,' Julia had said.

'Gentle Jesus come,' Claire said softly,
'Through the clouds of grace.

We would be exceeding glad,
To see Thy beauteous face.'

It was her favourite prayer. Julia had made it up for a class assembly the previous year and Miss Denman had given her three stars for it. Julia was always getting stars. Her name on the merit board had three whole rows of stars after it, which was three times fifteen. Claire tried to work out that sum in her head but failed; three fives are twelve, but which figure did she put down and which did she carry and what did she do then? Perhaps she could manage it if she had paper and a pencil. Claire didn't have many stars. Only five times one. Sometimes she started a lesson, a number lesson perhaps, really determined to finish the exercise right through. But after a few sums she always felt very tired. It just got too boring. Joined-up writing was too boring as well. She didn't like doing the letters in the same way all the time, and she didn't think the letters liked it either. As soon as she put down a big R, for instance, it seemed to be begging her for loops and tails, and little o's seemed to want dots in the middle, or eyes, and then Miss Denman would say, 'Oh Claire,' and Julia and her best friend, Amanda Walters, would turn round and frown at her.

She said the prayer again. The part she liked best of all was 'clouds of grace,' though she wasn't absolutely sure what they were; grey clouds perhaps, but tinged with feathery streaks of palest rose pink.

Having pictured such clouds very vividly, she wasn't altogether sure whether she would be exceeding glad to see a face, even a beauteous face, looking through them. Wouldn't it be a bit spooky?

The unease she felt turned to a hard, gripping fear. 'Are you asleep?' she asked Julia. Her voice trembled like a voice left out in the cold.

Julia was fast asleep. The light from the landing shone in from the half-open door. Claire got up on one elbow to draw what comfort she could from her sister's nearness. She was beautiful as a princess. Even asleep she looked calm and rather disdainful. Julia would know the answer.

She leaned over towards her. 'What's happened to John Hedward?' she asked her sleeping sister. 'Oh Julia, have you thought about John Hedward?'

She felt a little better even to have voiced the question. 'Julia, Julia,' she said very loudly, 'oh please, Julia, can I come into your bed?'

Julia woke just enough to say no.

There was complete silence in the room. No sound from any of the other children in their bedrooms, no sound from any of the grown-ups downstairs. No music from anywhere, no sawing or hammering, no friendly water gurgling in the pipes. No sound.

'All right,' Claire said at last, very, very softly. 'All right John Hedward, you can come in with me. That's it, you can come into my bed. That's a good little boy. You'll be warm in a minute. Are you comfortable? You want my teddy to hold? Here you are then. I'm too old for it now, you can have it. Good night, John Hedward, sleep tight. You shall be my little friend from now on.'

Hester and Louise

When I was a girl, women looked their age, particularly if they were widows. My grandmother could only have been in her early sixties when I remember her, but she had settled comfortably into old age; wiry grey hair scraped back into a tight bun, round cheeks reddened by sun and broken veins, dark shapeless clothes, grey woollen stockings baggy round the ankles.

She'd once been a district nurse. On the mantelpiece in the parlour, there was a photograph of her standing importantly at someone's front door, large bag in hand, round hat pulled down to the eyebrows, but I found it difficult to believe in this starched image, could only see the untidy old woman she'd become; shooing the hens away from the back door with a dirty tea cloth, bending to cut a lettuce in the garden, her large bottom in the air, or her most typical pose, standing at the gate, squinting into the sun, her big heavy breasts supported on her folded arms.

I stayed with her for five or six weeks every summer, not for her benefit or for mine, but because it eased the pressure on my parents who kept a dairy in St John's Wood.

I liked London far better than the Welsh countryside. I missed the Friday evening dancing class, the Saturday morning cinema, the big public library which was only two streets away and my friends, Jennifer and Mandy.

There was no dancing class, cinema or library in Brynawel and the village children scorned me. The much praised fresh air always seemed to have an overlay of cows' shit; I much preferred stale air with petrol fumes.

I didn't like Gran's meals either; runny boiled eggs with orange yolks for breakfast, dirty looking potatoes, greens and grey meat for dinner, rough brown bread with cheese and salad for supper, with the occasional addition of caterpillar or little black flies.

I didn't like my bedroom although it had once been my father's; the bed was hard, the pillows lumpy and the sheets coarse. But worst of all, my grandmother had no bathroom and expected me to strip-wash in the back kitchen with carbolic soap and the same wet towel she'd used. The summer when I was twelve, she promised to keep out when I was washing, but twice she forgot and came barging in and once the coalman came to the door and saw me in vest and knickers. 'Oh, the man will never be the same again,' was all she said when I complained.

When I was thirteen, I begged my parents to let me stay home; pleaded and cried, promising to serve in the shop, wash dishes, even peel potatoes. 'I'll do anything, anything, but please don't send me away to Gran's.'

My father thought I was mad. He and his brother Bob had had an idyllic childhood, he said; all the freedom of the fields and woods, fishing, ratting, scrumping apples, helping the farmers with the harvest, earning sixpence a day. 'This one's a girl though, Isaac,' my mother said. 'She likes different sorts of things, girls' things, going round Woolworths and the market, buying shampoo, trying on lipsticks, things like that. Try to understand.'

'It's not just those things,' I said, since he was looking at me as though he'd never seen me before. 'It's just that Gran doesn't have a bathroom, so I don't have any privacy. And I'm not a child any more. I have my periods now and I have to wear a bra. And I'm not going to bath in a back kitchen and you shouldn't expect me to.'

That shut him up. He could never tolerate any talk of bodily functions. And my mother promised to write a polite letter to Gran, explaining how I felt.

We had a letter back by return of post.

She quite understood the position. I was going through a little phase, that was all, and they were not to worry. She'd spoken to Hester and Louise, the Arwel sisters, though, and I was most welcome to use their bathroom any time I wanted to, twice a day if I'd a mind. And they, as I probably remembered, had an all-pink bathroom the size of a small ballroom with bottles of this and that and loofahs and sponges and a special brush for scrubbing your back, pale grey carpet on the floor and a little fluffy cover on the W.C.

'The Arwel sisters,' my father said, casting his eyes to the ceiling.

'I'll go,' I said. 'I love Miss Hester and Miss Louise. The Sundays they invite me to their house after church are the only days I enjoy.'

'She's a girl, Isaac,' my mother said again. 'Try to understand.'

Miss Hester and Miss Louise didn't seem to belong in Brynawel, but to a world I knew only from the cinema. I'd often try to describe them to my friends, Jennifer and Mandy. 'No, they're not really young, perhaps thirty-five or so, and they're like ladies in old-fashioned films with tiny waists and delicate faces like flowers. Well, I think they may have had sweethearts once, but perhaps they were killed in the war. No, they're definitely not spinsters, spinsters are altogether different. No, they don't have jobs, they just have money, plenty of money, so they can do whatever they want to. Sometimes they hire a car to take them out shopping or to the seaside or to church on Sunday. Otherwise they stay at home doing tapestry, reading magazines and changing their clothes. Oh, they're very gentle and kind. Just think of me going there each day! And I know they'll give me home-made lemonade and iced biscuits every time. I'm really looking forward to staying with Gran this year.'

The sisters called on the very afternoon I arrived, to remind me of their promise. 'Isn't she pretty,' one said, smoothing down my rough curly hair. 'Isn't she pretty,' the other replied. They always repeated each other's pronouncements. 'Hasn't she grown tall and slender.' 'Hasn't she grown tall and slender.'

'Don't turn her head,' Gran said. 'She's foolish enough already.'

'We've heard different. We've heard that she had an excellent end of term report and that she's a marvellous little pianist.'

'A marvellous little pianist, as well.'

'We want her to play for us. We've had our piano tuned.'

'We've had our old piano tuned specially.'

I'd forgotten the way they so often stood with their arms clasped tightly round each other's waists, as though they wanted to be one person instead of two.

They were dressed that day in cream high-necked blouses, full dark green skirts, black belts pulled tight and cream high-heeled shoes. They always dressed identically, though they weren't twins. Hester was a year and a half older and she was also a little taller and perhaps a little more elegant. Louise's eyes were a brighter blue, though, and her lips were fuller. I could never decide who was the more beautiful.

'Well, I must ask you to go now,' Gran said, 'because I always listen to my serial at four o'clock. I'll send the girl round after supper.'

I could never understand how Gran had the nerve to treat them so casually, even rudely, when she was ugly and poor and they were so beautiful and so rich.

'Who told them about my report?' I asked her when they'd left.

'I did, of course. I told them you were going to college to be a teacher. In case they have any ideas of turning you into a lady's maid.'

'Are they so rich?'

'Oh yes. Their father had the best farm in the county, but when he knew he was dying and with no son and heir, he had to sell it all, land and livestock, to buy an annuity for those two. Their mother had died, you see, when they were toddlers; soon after Louise was born, and he spoiled them, of course, and everybody spoiled them. Even when they were schoolgirls, they never had to do a hand's turn for themselves, let alone anything in the house or the farm. It was hard on him in the end. But what could he expect? He'd brought them up to be butterflies.'

'Why didn't they get married?'

'No one from round here was stupid enough to ask them, I suppose. To tell you the truth, your uncle Bob seemed to be thick with them at one time, but he never seemed to know which one of them he liked best and then he was called up and met your Auntie Dilys, so he lost them both.

'He was a born farmer, Bob was, ready to do a day and a half's work every day. Their father would have been proud to have him as a son-in-law, and he would have been the making of those girls, but which one of them?'

'But which one of them?'

'God help us, if you're going to start being an echo like those two.'

'God help us,' I began. But she cuffed me on the head and turned the wireless on.

To think that one of them could have been my auntie. My Auntie Dilys was nice enough, but she wasn't special in any way.

If I hurried over my supper and the washing up, I had two whole hours to spend at Arwel and I savoured every moment.

I'd be shown first into the drawing-room where we'd have

coffee, real coffee, served in a silver coffee pot, where I sat in a fat velvet chair and was passed a cup and saucer of green and gold eggshell china, pink crystals of sugar and exotic dark chocolates. After this delightful ritual, I might look at their photograph albums; two plump little girls sitting together on a garden seat, chubby legs and solemn round faces, two young girls in frilly party dresses with ribbons in their hair, two young ladies in their first ball gowns.

'This one is you, isn't it Hester?' I'd ask.

'Wait a minute, now. I really can't tell. No one seemed sure, even at the time. They always called us the girls or the sisters, you know, never our names. We hardly knew ourselves which of us was which, did we Louise?'

'We hardly knew ourselves, did we, Hester?'

The house was so beautiful, so wickedly luxurious; thick carpets everywhere and floor-length velvet curtains, heavy as the falling darkness outside. They lent me a dressing-gown of plum-coloured chenille and after I'd bathed and washed my hair, they'd take me to their bedroom and take it in turn to brush my hair, brushing gently, gently, almost as though they were in a trance. They each had an ivory hairbrush, I remember, one with a silver H on its back, the other an L. I wished my hair was long and straight and raven-black instead of short and reddish-brown. Gran had forbidden me to use make-up, but they insisted that complexion milk didn't count, so they smoothed it into my face and my neck and my shoulders. It felt soft and silky and smelt of little white roses and purple violets, so different from Gran's carbolic soap. 'She's got such delicate skin, hasn't she Hester?' 'Her skin is as soft as a baby's, isn't it, Louise?' Afterwards I was encouraged to try on their perfumes – luckily Gran had lost her sense of smell – and I loved repeating their grand French names; *Je Reviens, Bal de Nuit, Ma Griffe, L'Air du Temps, Mon Désir, Arpège.*

Their house had several bedrooms, six or seven I should think, but they slept together in the largest and grandest one in the front. (The long small room at the back of the house was where their maid, housekeeper, cook slept, a bustling little woman called Gwladys who had been with them since their birth. They always got her to walk home with me, but she never came very far because she was frightened of the dark and I wasn't.)

They slept in a high, old-fashioned bed with a brass bedstead. The quilt was a bright turquoise silk, the colour matching the tiny rosebuds on the cream wallpaper, and the carpets, the heavy curtains and the satin lampshades were a deep, voluptuous pink. There was a highly polished bedside table on either side of the wide bed with a framed photograph on each.

One evening Hester picked up the photograph from her side, gazing at it as though willing me to notice it. I didn't need much prompting. 'What a handsome man,' I said. He was handsome; dark curly hair, slanting eyes, straight nose and full, curved lips. And as I might have guessed, Louise then brought me the photograph from her bedside, and at first I thought it was the same man in a different pose.

'Brothers,' I said then. 'Twin brothers.'

They smiled at each other, but didn't volunteer any information and I was too shy to ask.

One evening towards the end of my holiday, though, when it was mothy and dark as Gwladys walked me back to Gran's, I ventured to ask her about the handsome young men.

She seemed flustered. 'What young men?'

'The brothers in the photographs on the bedside tables.'

'Yes. Very nice young gentlemen,' she said then. 'Sons of a very good family. Not from round here at all.'

'What happened to them?'

'Killed in the war.'

'Both of them?'

'Both of them. Nice young men. Real gentlemen. Not from these parts, of course.'

'Poor Miss Hester and Miss Louise.'

'Yes indeed. 1944. Ten years ago now, very near. And never anyone else after.'

'Gran told me that my Uncle Bob was friendly with them once.'

She was furious. 'Nonsense. Your Uncle Bob was a labourer. He worked on the farm but he never came to the house. He knew his place, Bob did. Your Gran likes to boast, that's all. I'm turning back now. You can run from here, can't you.'

'Gwladys *was* in a stew when I told her about Uncle Bob courting the sisters,' I told Gran.

'She knows nothing about it. She was in Swansea nursing her mother during the war. It was I who had to look after the sisters then.'

'Do you mean when their young men were killed?'

'Their young men? What young men are you talking about now?'

'Real gentlemen, Gwladys said they were. Sons of a very good family.'

'Gwladys is getting soft in the head.'

Now that I had my interesting association with the Arwel sisters to sustain me, Gran didn't seem so much of a trial; indeed she often seemed nothing but a fairly harmless relic from an unhygienic past. Sometimes in the evening, I sat at her side on the old rexine sofa, leaning my head on her shoulder, almost able to ignore the dirty dishcloth smell coming from her.

'Tell me a secret, Gran.'

'What about?'

'You know. About the sisters. About their past. Tell me why they're different from other people.'

'I'll tell you when you're older.'

'Gran, you'll be dead when I'm older.'

She chuckled at that. She liked straight talk. She leaned forward, looked me straight in the eye and cleared her throat. 'They never had any men friends, real gentlemen or otherwise. They only had one man between them and he . . . he was an Italian prisoner of war.'

'Is that all?'

'Isn't that enough?'

'He was a handsome man, anyway. I saw his photo, two of

his photos.'

'Married, of course.'

'So they were in disgrace, is that it?'

'You could say that, yes.'

I could see her hesitating about going on, but I squeezed her arm and gave her an imploring look.

'Their father found him in bed with them, you see. In between them, he said. That seemed to be the last straw. I don't think he'd have minded quite so much if he'd been either firmly on one side or the other, but there he was cuddled up between them. All three of them naked as babies, he said.'

'Naked?' I swallowed hard. Of course I knew about sexual intercourse, but I found certain of the details very unsavoury.

'Naked as new born babies.'

'And after the war, I suppose he went back to Italy?' I tried to keep the quiver out of my voice.

Gran paused again. 'No. No, sometime later he was found shot in Henblas woods.'

'Murdered? Do you mean murdered?'

'That's right. Murdered. The Italians weren't exactly loved at that time, especially the very handsome ones. No one found out who'd shot him. There were no clues. It could have been anybody, I suppose.'

'I think it was their father don't you, Gran, who murdered him.'

'It could have been their father. He had a massive heart attack six months later. It could have been guilt, I suppose.'

'Poor things. Poor Hester. Poor Louise.'

'Don't cry. You wanted the truth and now you must accept it.'

'And you had to look after them. Were they very unhappy?'

'They were, of course. Very unhappy.'

She glanced at me again, as though wondering how much more I could take. 'Go on,' I said.

'And pregnant as well. Very pregnant. Five or six months pregnant.'

'Both of them?'

'Both of them. Well, that's what happens when you lie naked in bed with a handsome young man, especially an Italian.'

'Both of them pregnant?'

'That's right.'

'Oh Gran, whatever happened to their little babies?'

'I looked after their babies, one boy, one girl, until they were old enough to be adopted. And it was straight after that their father died.'

'Gran, it's a terrible story, a cruel story.'

'That's why I didn't want you to hear it.'

We were both silent for a while. I felt there was a hand twisting my stomach. I wanted to be sick, wanted to vomit up everything I'd heard.

'But they've still got each other, haven't they,' I said at last.

'Yes, they've still got each other, God help them, foolish as they are.'

I thought of them, their arms tightly clasped round each other's waists, repeating each other's sentences, spending hours laying out their dresses on the wide bed deciding which to wear, trying on their lovely jewellery.

'Shall I spend the whole day with them tomorrow, Gran? Because it's my last day? They said I could.'

'Then I suppose you can. Silly girl. Go to bed now. You can come again next year . . . unless I'm dead before that, of course.'

I bent to kiss her good night. 'Silly girl,' she said again.

A House of One's Own

I'm Liverpool really, proper Scouse, but I've lived here in Brynhir – Brynhir, Gwynedd, North Wales – for nearly three months.

I own this house, this garden and that little stunted tree by the back wall.

Plenty of people own houses, I know, but for me it's a near-miracle because I've never owned anything before, a bag or two of clothes, a box of kitchen stuff, that's about it really.

When I got the letter from the solicitor I was struck dumb for a whole morning. I wanted to shout out the news to Anna Marie and Gina and Scottish Joe, the guys that shared the lousy flat I was living in, but I had no voice, not even a Scouse croak.

I was the sole legatee, the letter said, of Mr Trefor Roberts, 12 Clydwen Row, Brynhir, Gwynedd, and I could, at my convenience, pick up the key to the said property from Jenkins and Hedges, Solicitors, Hill Road, Caernarfon, Gwynedd.

Mr Trefor Roberts was my uncle Trefor, my great-uncle Trefor.

I could just about remember him. He visited us once when I was small. I think he only stayed a couple of days, probably because our house was a proper shambles, full of lodgers and wet washing, but for years after he used to send my Mum a ten shilling note every week, fastened to his letter by a neat little gold safety pin, and that didn't half make a difference to our life.

My father, my real father, also called Trefor Roberts, was his nephew. He married my mother straight after coming out of the army in 1946, his boat docked in Liverpool and he never went back to Wales after. I was born in 1951, the only child. He died of pneumonia when I was about two, and a bit after my mother married my step-dad who was the only father I can remember.

My great-uncle worked in one of these local quarries, I don't know which one, and when he came to visit us – well over thirty years ago – he already seemed old. Perhaps it was the heavy black suit he wore and the shiny black boots. He took me to the Sally Army Hall in Toxteth Road and I remember how loud he sang too. I think that was the only time he took me out, but he must have liked me a bit to leave me his house. Or I was his only living relative most like.

I've been thinking about him a hell of a lot since being in Brynhir, though of course I never gave him a thought before. Here, sleeping in his bed with the lumpy green and fawn mattress, sitting in his sagging old armchair, eating at his little scrubbed table, he seems almost alive and I wish I knew a bit more about him. He's got a little shelf of books, but I can't fuckin' read them because they're all in Welsh – people speak Welsh around here. But he wrote his diaries in English, so I've been looking through those. I was quite excited to discover them, forty black diaries, Letts diaries, the sort with a little pencil in a groove at the side, all laid out in perfect order in the top drawer of his bedroom chest. Unfortunately they're totally boring, all about his work at the quarry, the times of the blasting and so on, and on Sundays, the name of the preacher at the chapel he used to go to, the text of the sermon and the grade he gave it, usually a B. I found myself longing for a really bad sermon, something to liven up his week, but there was never a C or a D. I suppose he was always too ready to think the best of everyone.

The other day I walked past the chapel he used to go to. Several of the chapels around here have been closed down and used as warehouses or arts-and-crafts places, but his, Bethel, is still a chapel, and though I've never had a religious thought in my head, I was quite pleased.

Why should I be spending my time reading this man's boring diaries and thinking about him? I'm totally fascinated by him, that's why. If he was a cannibal chief he couldn't be more different from anyone I know; so quiet, so methodical, so tidy, so decent.

My next door neighbour, a cross old woman called Netta Morris, scrubs her step every day and when it's not raining I go out to see if she'll deign to speak to me. Usually she'll only mutter a grudging g'morning, but once or twice she's managed to part with a scrap of information. 'Mr Roberts was a good neighbour,' she said on one occasion. 'He always carried my ash-can out the back.'

'Why did he never get married?'

'He had no need. Could do everything for himself. Cooking, washing, ironing, even mending.'

'Didn't he need a bit of company? A bit of comfort?'

She went back into her house at that question, closing the

door firmly behind her.

I've always needed lots of company, lots of comfort. My mother was the same, but I'm worse. I've always needed lots of men and lots of booze, but for three months I've had neither. Being a property owner in Brynhir has filled my brain so that I don't need anything else, but it won't last. One of these days I'll pick up my giro, go down the pub on the pull and fill the house with men and loud sexy music and to hell with Netta Morris.

Last week I bought a large, dark green waterproof coat which cost twenty-three pounds. I could hardly believe what I was doing. I've never before owned such a remarkably boring and hideous garment. Oh yes, I know it will be useful – it doesn't stop raining in this place – and practical too because it will hide all the tat underneath, but since when have I gone in for being dry and respectable? Perhaps it's due to losing so much weight; I'm almost human-shaped now, what with giving up the booze and the Chinese takeaways. I also bought a window cleaner called Mr Brite and some new bags for Uncle Trefor's old Hoover. Am I becoming a fuckin' housewife?

I've got to the 1959 diary and discovered that in March that year Uncle Trefor was faced with a problem. The owner of his house, a Richard Paul Mathias, died, leaving it to two of his cousins who are in dispute over the will so that he doesn't know who to send the rent to. In April he went to Caernarfon to take advice from a Mr Stanley Jenkins, solicitor, who tells him not to send it to anyone until the matter has been settled.

I'm in a cold sweat. Do the cousins of Richard Paul

Mathias still own this house? Will I discover that this damp three-roomed terraced house – one room up, one room down and lean-to kitchen – is not really mine? I rush to the 1960 diary only to find that on January the first, my Uncle Trefor is still reporting that Mr Jenkins has advised him not to offer anyone the rent until it's demanded, but to keep the house in a good state of repair.

I'm too bloody agitated to read through the accounts of Sunday sermons and quarry blastings after that.

And it's that afternoon that the Reverend comes to call, the Reverend Dilwyn Owen, Bethel, a short, fat, jolly-looking man, about sixty years of age. 'I've given you plenty of time to settle in,' he says at the door, smiling a lot.

'I'm not one of the saved,' I tell him. 'I'm a big, bad sinner, I'm afraid. An alcoholic, for one thing.' Even as I say it, I realize it's not strictly true. I've hardly had a single drink in the last three months and when I went to The Bell last Friday night I only had two halves.

'Then you need friends,' he says.

I give him some brownie points for that. The holy joes usually say they'll fuckin' pray for me. 'Come in.' He's the first person to cross the threshold.

'It's a tidy little cottage,' he says. 'Mr Roberts always kept it nice and you the same.'

'You knew him well? The old man?'

'No one knew him well, but I knew him as well as anyone, I think.'

'Sit down,' I said, pointing to Uncle Trefor's armchair.

'Will you have a cup of tea?' Three months in this place and I'm offering cups of tea to elderly men in dog collars.

'I'll sit and talk, anyhow. I had a cup of tea half an hour ago. I'm getting fat on religious tea.'

'I want to ask you something. Only it's not to do with God.'

'Fire away. It's the God questions I'm frightened of.'

'Did my uncle really own this house? I've been reading his diaries and it seems to me that his landlord's cousins are the real owners.'

'I can put your mind at rest about that. Mr Roberts owned this house. The court granted him the title deeds because he'd maintained it in good order and repair for over twenty years.'

'And that's legal?'

'Perfectly legal. I've got the facts at my fingertips because I often use it as a text for my sermons. It has a great moral significance in my opinion, who owns Wales, for instance, who are the rightful inheritors. But I won't bore you with politics. Suffice it to say, you own this house.'

'I'm very grateful to you. It saves me a trip to Caernarfon and a lot of worry.'

'There we are. What are friends for? Incidentally, do you know what Mr Roberts did with his rent money every week?'

'Used it to maintain the property, you said.'

'He did maintain the property, certainly, but that ten shillings rent he used to send to your mother every week.'

'I remember it arriving every week like clockwork. Ever

after that time he came to visit us.'

'Do you know why he visited her? At that time? The only time he ever went further than Caernarfon?'

'No. Do you?'

'He'd read in a Sunday newspaper, *The News of the World* it might have been, that your stepfather had been murdered by some drunken fellows outside a local public house and he thought he should find out how your poor mother was taking it.'

'How she was taking it? Do you want the truth? She was over the bloody moon about it. And so was I. And so were all his bloody mates. Sorry about the lingo, Reverend.'

'Your stepfather wasn't a popular character?'

'He was a petty crook, a drunkard, a wife beater and a child molester.'

'He molested you?'

'Yes. He molested me.'

'I think I'll have that cup of tea. Thank you.'

Why shouldn't I tell the Reverend the truth? Let him know something about the real world out there? Yes, I was sexually abused, Reverend, from the age of – what? Three or four? And this at a time when social workers and their like weren't on the lookout for signs of it. No, I never told my mother. Not because I thought she'd turn against me or stop loving me, but because he told me he'd kill me if I did. Oh, I remember the way he'd kneel over me, pushing his fingers into me front and back, pretending it was fun and that I was supposed to laugh. 'I'm tickling you,' he used to say. And then he'd get his big prick out and hurt me real bad and when

I cried he'd say, 'Tell her and I'll kill you.' And when he got his trousers back on, he'd take a knife out of his pocket and stand over me, stroking the blade of it.

I was nine or ten when he was killed. Some neighbours from the estate and the pub got up a collection for my Mum and the day after the funeral we went on the train to a fairground at West Kirby and we went on the Big Dipper over and over again until all the money was gone, shouting out with terror and joy. I didn't tell that bit to the Reverend, but that's what we did. Joy, joy, joy.

My Mum was a big woman like me. She was around forty by this time and she drank a lot and had lots of men friends, but we had quite a good sort of life for the next ten years. Lots of rows and shouting, specially when I got to be thirteen, fourteen, and wanting my own way about everything, but lots of fun and rowdy parties and really great celebrations for birthdays and Christmas.

She died at fifty – cancer – and after that I took over where she left off, work at the factory Monday to Friday and boozing and men at the weekend. And all the men were rough and greedy and easy to hate. There was no way I could admire or love a man was there? The memories of being used and abused stay with you.

The bloody diaries seem to be all I've got. After the quarry shut down, he often left his weeks completely blank except for the Sunday sermons, always Bs. Then in 1986 he starts to write a chirpy little slogan for every week which shows he's softening up but they stop abruptly in February 1987. In fact the diary stops altogether in

May 1987. I wonder if he went blind? Or lost his marbles? Who looked after him from 1987 until he died in March this year? Would Netta Morris be likely to tell me? Probably not.

On Friday I go to the corner shop for my groceries. 'This is the tea Mr Roberts liked,' the woman behind the counter tells me.

So she knows who I am. Nosey cow.

I ignored her and bought a different brand. But then I relented. 'Did you know him well?' I asked her. 'He was my great-uncle, but I only met him once.'

'He was a very private man. Didn't speak much to anyone.'

'Who looked after him at the end?'

'He was active to the last, chopping firewood, digging his garden, doing his shopping, chapel of course every Sunday. Didn't smoke or drink. Not much of a life. Wouldn't do for me, I can tell you.'

I looked at her with new interest. 'Didn't I see you in The Bell last week?'

'That's right. My girl-friend and I were hoping you might join us but you left without as much as a glance our way.'

'Will you be there tonight?'

'We're there most nights.'

'See you tonight, then.'

'See you tonight. By the way, do you play darts?'

'Only when I'm sober.'

'Ta-ra then. See you tonight.'

Things are looking up around here. My new friend seems lively enough. Perhaps she'll introduce me to some decent man and a whole new decent way of life. Huh! Perhaps we'll have a few jars and a laugh together anyway.

'You got a husband?' I ask her.

'Yeh, we don't get on. You?'

'No, I don't have that grief. Any kids?'

'Three.'

'I got three kids too. They took them away from me though. They're in this home in Moorfields.'

'That's awful. How did that happen, then?'

'Couldn't stop drinking, that was my trouble.'

'Gets you like that sometimes.'

'Got me like that. Couldn't stop it. Seem to have snapped out of it now, though. Practically on the wagon.'

'You've got something behind you now. Nice little house. Makes all the difference. Try and get them back.'

'I think about it. But I don't know. They've been back that many times. No one believes in me any more.'

'I believe in you, kid. I know how hard it is. There's lots around here know how hard it is, coping with life with next to nothing coming in.'

'I had a good job once.'

'They're wanting chambermaids in the Maesgwyn Arms. That's a good job.'

'I've got no references, though. Nothing up to date.'

'You won't need them. Just tell them who you are. Mr

Trefor Roberts's great-niece. Everybody knew him. You've got it made. When you've got a job and a house, you'll get them kids back. How old are they?'

'The girl's fifteen, two boys, nine and eight. The girl's a bit of a problem, though, one way or another.'

'Course she is. So's mine. Mine's sixteen and she was a proper little tearaway. But now she's got a job up Llandudno way, country house hotel, living in, and she comes home on her day off, sunny as you like. You go and see about the job. Things will work out for you in this place, you mark my words. Have another drink.'

'Just one more then.'

The next morning I have a hell of a hangover and I'm quite pleased about it too. I had a good night out with a new friend and things seem brighter. Maybe I'll go to the Maesgwyn Arms and maybe they'll give me a job on account of my uncle's famed respectability and maybe I'll contact the authorities and maybe I'll get my kids back and maybe we'll manage, as he did, keeping things in good order and repair. For years and years and years. Being bored and bored and bored. Is that all there is to life? I'll have to ask the Reverend. I don't think he'll fob me off with fairy tales. I don't want to be respectable, Reverend, just half-way decent.

Netta Morris knocks at my door. 'You woke me up coming in so late last night,' she says, 'and all that noise. Your uncle never disturbed me in fifty years.'

'Pity he didn't disturb you a bit. I bet you were a good-looking lass fifty years ago.'

'You mind your own business.'

'You want a cup of tea?'

She thinks about it crossly and then comes in. 'Your uncle never asked me in in fifty years,' she says.

'Silly old sod,' I say.

Mountain Air

My mother was always happy when she was with her sister, my Auntie Phyllis; she seemed younger too, and much more fun. She and my Auntie Phyllis talked about the time when they were girls, and the world, then, seemed a much brighter place. Their father was a builder with his own business, there was money to spend and he enjoyed spending it, particularly on his pretty daughters.

'Of course we left school at fourteen,' my mother would say. 'I suppose he should have sent us to the County.'

'Whatever for? I was happy enough in my job, weren't you?'

'I suppose so. But I would have liked . . .'

'Of course you were. We never paid a penny for our keep, we always had money for clothes, and what we couldn't afford we could wheedle out of him. Oh, we had a grand time, dancing every Saturday night, the tennis club, the operatic society. Do you remember *The Gondoliers*? Do you remember how many encores we had for 'Three Little Maids from School'?'

I loved it when they got up and put their arms on each other's shoulders and started dancing and singing. They were both plump, my Auntie Phyllis very plump.

'I'm out of condition, Katie,' she'd say at last. 'Just look at me. A stone and a half surplus.'

'Ah, but it's in all the right places,' my mother would reply, planting her hands firmly on her sister's bountiful hips. And they'd both laugh again.

I loved hearing about all the films they'd seen. 'They knew how to make films those days, a real good story, none of this fancy stuff.' Sometimes one would start unravelling the intricacies of the plot, the other would interrupt her and carry on, but somehow they never got to the end. 'Do you remember the woman in the one-and-nines who was forever turning round to tell us what was coming next? She used to go to the pictures every night of the week and sometimes the Saturday matinée as well. She smelt of mothballs. Her face was dead white. Someone said she put flour on it.'

'She was a nice old thing, though. She sometimes gave us mintoes.'

'They tasted of mothballs.'

'Didn't we laugh?'

Most of their anecdotes ended like that. 'Didn't we laugh?' They'd had some good times.

I knew everything about their lives when they were young; their adventures with Will Jenkins, bus conductor, and Charlie Smith, commercial traveller, the wonderful summer when they'd had a college student each. 'From Aber they were, and doing Teacher Training in the County. We met them in the clubhouse, didn't we Katie, and right from the start Jim Parry fancied you and Bob Howells fancied me.' She sighed. 'So often it worked out wrong, the one I liked, liked you, the one you liked, liked me, but that time we were all happy. Do you remember that handsome park-attendant we met at one of the summer concerts? The one with the shoulders? What was his name? Ken something, if I remember right. But do you remember that little runt he brought along with him the next Saturday? Which one of us was he meant for, I wonder? We just drank our shandies and disappeared round the back.'

'Ken Williams,' my mother said, with a touch of sadness, 'Ken Williams. That was his name.'

I felt sure he'd liked her best. It was in her voice.

I often wondered how they'd ended up with my Uncle Jack and my father; my father an insurance collector with very little sense of humour and my Uncle Jack a small-time painter and decorator who drank too much.

I suppose I was the only one who paid any attention to their reminiscences. They had eight children between them, four each, but I was the only girl. The boys liked to be out kicking a ball whenever they got together; except for Bobby, Auntie Phyllis's youngest, who was still a baby.

We didn't get to see each other very often, but every year in the summer holidays we had a day out in the mountains. Our family lived in the town so that we had further to travel, my Auntie Phyllis's family lived in a village nine miles up the valley so they were almost half-way there.

The trip took a lot of organization. Neither family had a phone, so that arrangements like, 'the first fine day next week,' were fraught with suspense and danger. A day which began cloudy or even rainy might clear up in a few hours, but would Auntie Phyllis have listened to the forecast?

I loved the bus journey up the valley, between gentle meadows and little wooded hills, but couldn't settle to be happy until I saw the other family waiting in Pontgoch. Yes, there they were, Michael and the twins out in the middle of the road, waving their bags at the driver, in case he shouldn't notice my very plump auntie and Bobby flagging him down at the bus-stop. (I loved my cousin Michael, but he didn't take much notice of me because he was so much older; big and tall and stern-looking.)

Other passengers would move to other seats so that we could all sit together, congratulating one another on the cloudless sky and comparing picnic food. 'I've got corned beef sandwiches for dinner, ham sandwiches for tea, four packets of custard creams and four bottles of pop,' my Auntie Phyllis would say. She always had white bread and butter and lovely shop jam, while my mother had brown bread, home-made jam and home-made cake. Our food was left till last.

I took Bobby on my lap. The others could go off and do whatever stupid things they chose as long as I had Bobby. 'Can I carry him? Can I carry him?' I begged, as soon as we got off the bus.

'No, let him walk a little way, Megan. You shall give him a piggy-back when he's tired.'

'Upp-a. Upp-a.' Bobby said, holding out little fat arms, and of course I hoisted him up there and then.

The mountains were lovely, green and round-backed, the heat-haze just lifting. 'Well, here we are,' my Auntie Phyllis always said as soon as we'd walked a few yards from the road. 'This is Wales, isn't it boys. This is where we belong.'

'When I leave school I'm going to Birmingham,' Ifor, one of the twins said. 'Aston Villa for ever!'

'Give us a song, Gareth,' my mother said quickly. The smaller of the twins had a prize-winning treble voice.

'Give us a song, choirboy,' the other boys chanted.

'Now don't start fighting till you've put your bags down. I don't want any broken bottles. Remember last year.'

At last we reached the ideal picnic spot; the ground almost flat, large boulders for back-rests, a trickling stream, not too many sheep droppings and the road still visible, a winding silver thread far below us; my mother liked to be in sight of the road.

I think I must have been eight or nine the year we missed the bus back; my brothers and cousins all in their teens except for Bobby, nearly two.

We ate and drank soon after midday and after a story-telling contest which my eldest brother won, the big boys ran off to explore and I was left to play with Bobby.

He was a good-natured, contented baby, very easy to amuse. I only had to put one of his little toys on my head and tip it off and he'd laugh as though it was the greatest trick in the world. I suppose I carried on doing that for half an hour. Afterwards I recited nursery rhymes, tickled his little fat belly, kissed and cuddled him until at last he fell asleep and Auntie Phyllis laid him down in the cropped grass with her cardigan over him.

'Are you going to find the boys now?' she asked me.

'No, I've got a book to read.'

'Aren't you a clever one. Not one of mine has ever read a book. Not from choice, anyhow.'

I opened my library book, but only pretended to read. It was much more interesting to listen to the conversation going on behind me. My mother and Auntie Phyllis weren't speaking now about the golden days when they were young, but about their present lives. They spoke softly, almost in whispers at times, but I could follow most of it. I kept my eyes on my book, but my ears attuned to them.

Perhaps they suspected that I was eavesdropping; Auntie Phyllis referred to Uncle Jack as Mr Plum and my mother called my father the Reverend.

'Have I told you about the time Mr Plum stayed out till stop-tap and his poor wife put his supper down in front of him, telling him off a bit, I daresay, and what did he do but turn his plate head over tip onto the clean tablecloth and get himself some bread and cheese. "Take that away," he said to his wife after. "Clear that up." "Not on your life," she said. "There it stays as far as I'm concerned and if you don't take it away, there it'll be for your children to see in the morning." '

'What happened?' my mother asked, a thrill of fear in her voice.

'The poor woman went to bed eventually and when he

came up at last he said in a low voice, yes, he had cleared it up. "And did you rinse out the cloth?" she asked him. "Did I hell," he said and with that he cracked his shin against the side of the bed and went hopping about on one leg, making such a to-do that she couldn't help laughing at him. And in the end he started to laugh too, and that was the end of that.'

'The Reverend is so tight-fisted, Phyllis. His poor wife has to account for every penny. You wouldn't believe how she's got to scrimp and save before the family can have any little treat. Every week he has to have something put by for the children's education. I suppose he means well and it might be worth it in the end, but meanwhile his poor wife can't afford to have her shoes mended. Never a penny for any new clothes.'

'At least he doesn't drink, Katie.'

'He's too mean to drink, girl. Too mean to have any vices.'

'Mr Plum's got plenty. One of them works behind the bar of the Red Lion.'

'You don't mean it.'

'Cross my heart. A common piece, too, big mouth and a skirt up to her crotch. His wife goes in there with him the occasional Friday night. When she pulls the beer, she leans towards him showing everything she's got. On his birthday, when his sisters were down that time and we all went in for a drink, her behind the bar gave him such a long birthday kiss, everyone was counting and banging the bar and cheering.'

'Whatever did his wife do?'

'Pretended to laugh like everybody else. But the next

morning when the pub opened she went along to have a quiet word. Only the little tart was in her rollers with no make-up on and she felt sorry for her somehow. So she said she'd come in to ask whether they'd found her scarf, and they both searched for it, best of friends. And the next night he said, "I didn't know you'd lost your scarf, kid." "Who told you I had?" "Kim, the girl behind the bar." "And I suppose Kim is your little bit on the side?" she asks him. "Does a man need a little bit on the side when he's got a gorgeous piece like you at home?" he says, slapping her bottom.'

'At least they have their bit of fun. Mr Plum has his faults, yes, but I bet he gives his wife some good times. The Reverend is much too virtuous to enjoy himself, even going for a walk on a Sunday afternoon is wearing out shoe leather. Do you know when his poor wife last went to the pictures? Can you guess when she last had a holiday? Her father, God rest his soul, warned her that he was a dry old stick. Never trust a man in a dicky-bow, he used to say, and never trust a man with no faults.'

I didn't understand everything they said by a long way, but I got the gist of it; life wasn't easy even when you were grown-up – not if you were a woman anyhow. I sighed and turned over on my belly and started to count my afflictions: straight hair, freckles, not much good at sums, hopeless at rounders. And a girl as well.

I fell asleep.

When I woke up, Bobby was whining and my mother and my Auntie Phyllis were in a state about something and taking no notice of him. 'What's the matter?' I asked them.

'Give him a drop of lemonade, Megan,' Auntie Phyllis

said. 'That's right, and jig him up and down a bit, he's always fretful when he's slept too long.'

'What time is it?'

'Gone half past four, love, and those good-for-nothing lads not back for their tea. Quarter to four, I said, didn't I Katie? Don't be later than a quarter to four, I said over and over again. The bus goes at five past five and it's the only one. What if we miss it? We'd have to hire a car from somewhere and what about the expense? Michael would have to walk back to that hotel on the road to Tregroes and ask if he could use their phone.'

'I don't know what Meurig will say if we don't use our return tickets. He can't bear waste.'

'What's happened to them, that's what I'd like to know. They've never been late before, you know that. They're usually back before they've gone, their tongues hanging out for the rest of the lemonade.'

'Can I give Bobby some biscuits?'

'Yes, love, and have some yourself. There's some sandwiches too. Strawberry jam. Oh, what's happened to our children? Thank goodness we've got one each left, Katie. Do you feel like having a little run up to the brow of that hill, Megan, to see if you can catch a glimpse of them?'

'No, Phyllis, she's not to. As soon as you get to the top of one, there's another and another. I don't want her getting lost as well.'

'Well, what if we leave them here to find their own way back? What's a ten-mile trek to healthy youngsters? Six of them together, they'd have a great time. I could put yours to sleep with mine and send them back on the ten-fifteen tomorrow. Their tickets would probably be all right.'

'We . . . we can't leave them,' I said, bursting into tears.

'If we think about something else, they'll turn up,' my mother said. 'Let's have a game of I-Spy.'

'I spy with my little eye . . . Oh, don't be silly Katie. Look, why don't you three start walking down towards the road, I'll wait here to hurry them up when they arrive and you ask the bus driver to hang on a bit.'

'They've got to run according to the timetable, Phyllis. He wouldn't wait.'

'He'd wait five or ten minutes if you asked him nicely. He knows it's the last bus.' By this time, my Auntie Phyllis was morosely eating her way through the jam sandwiches.

'I'm ten years too old to ask him nicely.'

'No you're not. You flutter those eyelashes and let your mouth quiver a bit. You as well, Megan. You've got to learn sometime. Right, let's have a little rehearsal.'

'Let's all shout,' my mother suggested. 'If we all shout together perhaps they'll hear us.'

'What shall we shout?'

'Ice-cream. That would bring them.'

'Issceam,' Bobby said, spitting out his biscuit.

'Ice-cream', we shouted. 'Ice-cream. Ice-cream.'

'Now we've frightened those damn sheep. What a noise. Oh, let's all start walking down. Thank goodness most of the bags are empty. I'll take Bobby, Megan. In case you fall, love.'

We scrambled and stumbled down the side of the mountain, looking behind us every few minutes, feeling uneasy. It had become chilly. Clouds scurried by, casting their shadows over us. The mountains seemed full of menace.

We were still quite a distance from the road when we saw the bus passing by. To others it might seem a friendly old thing; a top speed of thirty miles an hour and noisy on the gear change, to us it was treacherous as a tiger. My mother sat down on a mossy stone, white with worry.

'Where are those sinners?' my Auntie Phyllis asked.

'Meurig will be meeting the bus,' my mother said. 'What will he have for his supper? I'd got him a nice piece of haddock, but I know he won't cook it himself.'

'He can get some fish and chips for once.'

'Oh, he won't do that Phyllis. Not after giving me the week's housekeeping.'

'Anyway it's those damned boys you should be worrying about. Meurig is safe enough.'

'Issceam,' Bobby shouted, waving back at where a posse of boys were whooping down the mountain.

Michael reached us first and my Auntie Phyllis clouted him round the head. 'We've missed the bloody bus,' she said. 'Where have you all been?'

'It's alright,' he said, rubbing his ear. 'We've been helping a farmer and he's going to bring his van and give us all a lift back.'

'Is he?' my mother asked. 'Is he really?' Oh, that's

something Phyllis, isn't it? But what have you been doing? We brought you up here for a day out on the mountains, not to help farmers.'

'There was a sheep got out on a ledge,' one of my brothers said. 'Been out there since Sunday, the farmer told us. And he was trying to get her back. But it was too dangerous for him to get down the ledge to get a rope round her. But Gareth did it.'

'Gareth did it?' my Auntie Phyllis screamed, shaking him and clouting him soundly.

'He's the smallest of us, Auntie, so there was less chance of him dislodging the stones.'

Gareth moved a judicious few yards from his mother. 'And I put the rope round her belly and tied it tight and then Mr Llywellyn and the boys hauled her up and after they got her safe, they threw the rope down to me and hauled me up.'

'Oh my Lord. You wait till your father hears about this. You risked your life. We bring you up here for a day out in the mountain air and you decide to go risking life and limb. What if you'd fallen down onto another ledge and been stuck there all night? Oh my Lord. What would poor Ifor have done if you'd been killed?'

'I'd have been OK,' Ifor said, at which my Auntie Phyllis lunged out and clouted him too.

'She breathed all over my face,' Gareth said. 'She knew I was rescuing her. She kept looking at me. Her eyes never blinked and her breath was hot as flame. She kept looking at me and breathing.'

'They're all safe, thank Heavens,' my mother said. 'And I suppose Gareth was very brave, even though he shouldn't have done it. Put your mother first, Gareth, in future. Doesn't your mother mean more to you than a silly sheep?'

'When is this man coming to fetch us?' my Auntie Phyllis asked, since Gareth seemed in no hurry to reply.

'He can't come till six because of the milking, but he's got a big van, he says, with plenty of room for us all.'

'And are you sure he'll come, Michael?' my mother asked. 'Do you trust him?'

Michael looked at her steadily. 'I do, Auntie. I trust him.'
Suddenly the tension lifted and the spell of the mountains was on us again. We had almost an hour to wait, but who cared. It was getting cold now, but we could still feel the sun-glow on our bodies and there were three packets of biscuits left and a full bottle of lemonade.

Gareth came out of his sulks and sang 'Yr Arglwydd Iôr', and 'Oh, for the Wings of a Dove', and then in the spotlight of the westering sun with the lovely mountains, blue and violet, as backdrop, my mother and my Auntie Phyllis went through their considerable repertoire of songs and dances.

Mr Llywellyn arrived soon after six and though my Auntie Phyllis had sworn to speak her mind to him about the danger to Gareth, she changed her mind when she found how concerned he was that we'd missed our bus, how apologetic about the goings-on of sheep, 'as okkard as women,' he said they were, and in no time she was laughing with him and poking him in the ribs.

He gave Gareth a ten-shilling note and all the rest of us, even Bobby, a two-shilling piece.

It was bumpy in the back of the van and you couldn't see out, but I was sitting next to Michael and after a while he showed me how to whistle with a piece of grass between your thumbs. And when at last I managed a little squeak, he said I was a jolly good sport.

When we got home, my father was standing by the empty grate looking very sorry for himself.

'You missed the bus,' he said mournfully. 'However did you get home?'

'We managed fine,' my mother said. 'You worry too much, Meurig, and you work too hard. You should have come with us to the mountains.'

And with that, she put her hands tightly round his waist and danced him round and round and round the spinning kitchen.

Outside Paradise

The house was very strange, the vast front room a jumble of books and magazines and shawls; there seemed a great number of shawls, over sofas and chairs, pinned up on the walls and just laid about anywhere. I looked about me with slight unease, knowing that my mother would be itching to tidy up.

Every house I'd been to before was more or less like our house, two small, square rooms with highly polished furniture, some carefully placed ornaments, usually copper or brass, a picture over the mantelpiece, mountains and lakes or woodlands in autumn. The size and exuberance of Genista's house took me by surprise. It seemed like a house in an old-fashioned book where they had maids and a nanny.

'Do you have a nanny?' I asked Genista, nervously wondering where she'd put my coat. I was beginning to feel out of my depth and wasn't sure I wanted to stay.

'Heavens no, do you?'

'Heavens no.'

I loved the way Genista talked. She never said 'everything' but 'every blessèd thing'. She said, 'Oh God', and 'Heavens above', and 'Saints alive', and 'Oh bloomin' heck'.

If I said 'Oh bloomin' heck', I'd be sent to my room. My mother had been a teacher before she'd got married and she insisted that my brother and I spoke properly. We weren't even allowed to say OK. My father was a fitter and turner on the railway. My mother clicked her tongue on the roof of her mouth at some of the things he said, 'Keep your hair on', 'I've got the gut-ache', 'I'm going to the dubs'. 'Oh Alfred,' she'd say, 'not in front of the children.'

'Let's find some grub,' Genista said. 'We won't do very well if we wait for the rest of the ravening hordes.'

She led me into a large kitchen which had a black-leaded range and a dresser and a big scrubbed table. It was a bit like my grandmother's kitchen, but much bigger. We had an electric stove, a green and chrome cabinet and a small formica-topped table. My mother was proud of her kitchen, it was labour-saving she said.

Genista opened some tins and shook out some biscuits and some pieces of Swiss roll onto a couple of shiny, dark blue plates. 'Do you like tea or drinking chocolate?' she asked me. 'Or shall I make both? I can easily make both.'

Before I'd replied, a tall, very thin woman fluttered into the room. I knew it wasn't Genista's mother because she'd been to school to see the Headmaster the previous week and we'd all stared at her. She was very pretty with a lovely smile.

'Oh Grace,' the tall woman said. 'Darling, if you're making tea could you possibly bring your father a cup?'

'I'm Genista and I'm only making drinking chocolate. Would a cup of drinking chocolate be OK?'

'I'll ask him.' She sidled out again, thin and silent as a shadow.

'Whoever was that?' I asked. I'd never seen such a thin and cold-looking woman. She was wearing a pale blue tunic which matched the colour of her nose and cheeks.

'Maud Illingsworth. She plays the oboe. She's supposed to be looking after father so why shouldn't she make his bloomin' tea?'

'Does your father play the oboe?'

'No, *she* does. Maud Illingsworth.'

'Where's your mother?'

'Probably working in the garden.'

When I had people to tea, my mother stood over them as she passed round fish-paste sandwiches, egg and cress sandwiches, chocolate biscuits and home-made fruit cake. 'Another cup of tea, dear?' she'd ask, her voice always polite even to Vera Hopwood who played with her food and dropped crumbs on the floor.

Genista had only recently moved to the village so she hadn't had one of my mother's teas.

She put two large yellow mugs on the table and poured rich, frothing hot chocolate into them. 'Right-ho,' she said. 'Tuck in. Sugar?' I'd never before had biscuits and cake without two pieces of brown bread and butter first. I put my elbows on the table and dipped my coconut-cream biscuits into my hot chocolate as Genista was doing. It was gorgeous.

'OK?' she asked.

'Oh yes. OK. Thank you.'

We'd finished the biscuits and were starting on the Swiss roll when Genista's mother came in through the back door. 'Hello

Valerie,' she said, taking off her muddy boots and smiling. 'I'm so glad you could come.'

'It's Betty,' Genista said. 'Valerie is Grace's friend.'

'Hello Betty. I'm so glad you could come.'

'Thank you for having me,' I said.

She scrubbed her hands at the sink, then filled the kettle and put it on the range.

'Maud Illingsworth came down wanting tea for father,' Genista said. 'But she couldn't be bothered to make any.'

'Lazy cow,' her mother said. And then she sat down in front of the range yawning for all she was worth. She didn't put her hand before her mouth either, but she looked lovely I thought, happy with herself like a cat. When she'd finished her very thorough yawning, she looked at us as though about to say something, but only smiled instead. I turned back to my lemon Swiss roll. Her eyes were yellow, not lemon-yellow but almost gold like a cat's. She heard someone at the door. 'Ah, here's Grace and Rosamund. Ready for a cup of tea, girls?'

Grace and Rosamund went to the grammar school in Newbridge and came home by bus. They were both tall and blonde with long straight hair and pale blue eyes. They took no notice of me, but I didn't expect them to. They were fifteen and sixteen.

'Say hello to Valerie,' their mother said.

They each lifted their eyes in my direction.

'Maud Illingsworth and father want some tea,' Genista said. 'We're going to watch 'Blue Peter'. Come on, Betty.'

I'd have preferred to stay in the warm kitchen to watch the

beautiful girls having tea with their beautiful mother who had gold-brown hair tied back in a large bun, a lovely smile and a man's blue shirt which showed a lot of soft white chest, but I followed Genista into a room she called the den.

I sank into a huge sofa, looking around at this second splendid room: I could watch 'Blue Peter' any old time. Here, there was a warm, spicy smell, wooden floors with rugs, velvet curtains, velvet cushions, and on the walls, big paintings everywhere instead of shawls. I got up to look at them more closely. They were all of dark-haired, foreign-looking women, some of them almost naked, some of them dressed as ballet dancers, Spanish dancers or acrobats. They were painted rather carelessly I thought, the black outlines much too thick, the pale pinks and mauves and blues of the skin and dresses running over the edges, the backgrounds hazy. But though I was scornful of the technique, I had to admit that they were definitely . . . not half bad. I walked round them again. Oh Heavens and Oh God, I said to myself, they're bloomin' beautiful, that's what they are. They were so bloomin' beautiful that tears filled my eyes and rolled down my cheeks. I never usually cried, at home or at school. What was happening to me in this house?

'Whatever's the matter with you?' Genista asked. 'Did you want to watch ITV? You should have said.'

I sniffed, 'I've got the gut-ache,' I said miserably.

'Do you want to go home?'

'No.' I didn't want to go home, ever.

'I like the pictures,' I said when I felt I could speak normally.

'Heavens above, do you really? I'll have to tell Father. Most people hate them. No one buys them. That's why we're so bloomin' poor.'

'Did your father paint them? Is he an artist?'

'Sort of, I suppose. Shall we go into the garden now?'

I followed her out through the french doors, down some steps and into the garden. It was already almost dark.

Genista's family had only been living in Glen Ross for just over a month so I knew her mother couldn't be entirely responsible for the lovely garden, but I felt it suited her, that it was the sort she would have planned. It was the sort of garden you saw in films about gardens; a soft shadowy green everywhere with narrow pathways pushing though the bushes and tall trees which went right round the house so that you hardly noticed it from the road. We had a small square lawn and a vegetable patch in the back.

'My mother's been planting bluebells along here,' Genista said. 'Five hundred bulbs.'

'Will I be able to come and see them?'

'Do you like flowers, then?'

'Yes. Don't you?'

'I suppose so.' Her voice was stern; I think she was beginning to suspect that I was soppy. 'Look, here's the old swing. Shall we have a go? Pretend we're kids?'

I pushed her on the swing, she pushed me and then I pushed her again. Her long straight pale-yellow hair gleamed in the dusk like pale seaweed. We stayed in the garden until it was completely dark and then felt our way back towards the bright lights of the house. There seemed to be a light in every window so that it looked like a house on a Christmas card.

We went in through the front door. I hadn't been that way before; the big square hall had brass-framed mirrors, pots of ferns and two glass lamps, one hanging above the other.

As I was wiping my feet on the doormat and looking round, Genista's eldest sister, Marigold, arrived home. I think she was eighteen. She looked just like the other girls except that she wasn't wearing school uniform but a tight red suit and a black satin blouse and her hair was tied back in a pony-tail.

'Hello girls,' she said. 'Has Bill arrived?'

'Haven't a clue,' Genista said. 'We've been in the garden.'

'That's her new boy-friend,' she added when Marigold had gone into the kitchen. 'Bill Bryden. Not too bad. Better than her usual type.'

'I know Bill Bryden. He lives near us.'

I suddenly felt hot and uneasy. Bill Bryden worked in the gas showroom in town. He was nice enough, small and dark and lively, but far too ordinary to have any sort of foothold in this house. He used to go out with a girl called Hilda Bainbridge, the sort of girl who made my mother sniff.

'He's in the Newbridge football team,' Genista said. 'Last Saturday we all went to the game. He scored a goal and we didn't half yell.'

'Did your mother go?'

'No. Just us four.'

I sighed my relief.

'Do you want to meet my father now?' Genista asked me. 'It's entirely up to you.'

'Oh gosh, yes.' I straightened my school tie and patted my hair down.

'He'll call you "young lady". You mustn't mind that.'

'Oh gosh, no.'

We went back into the room with shawls. There was a fire lit and loud music playing. Genista hurried over to the gramophone and turned down the volume.

Her father was quite old, more like a grandfather really, with a lot of grey hair and a grey beard. 'This is Elizabeth Miles, Father. She lives near the school in a house called 2 Edmund's Close.'

He turned to look at me. 'Have they given you any supper, Elizabeth?' he asked. 'Someone's cooking haddock but I haven't been offered any. Why don't you two cut along and see if you can bring me something on a tray. Anything will do, an egg or a piece of cheese. I won't expect haddock.'

'I'll go. Elizabeth can stay and talk to you. OK?'

I swallowed hard. 'OK.' I looked at the floor, then at him, then at the floor again. 'I like your paintings,' I said at last, 'They're not very neat, but . . . I do like them.'

He smiled, took my hand and raised it to his lips. I felt the dry, rough skin of his mouth and the roughness of his beard. He was an artist, a real artist.

I tried to think of something else to say. 'I'm really called Betty,' I said, 'but Genista feels sorry for me.'

He looked closely at me. 'Why?' he asked.

How could I explain?

'She told me you were a demon at sums and top of the class at composition.'

I felt myself blushing. 'Your paintings are really beautiful,' I said. Again I felt tears pricking my eyes.

Genista brought her father a smallish piece of haddock, some bread and butter and a cup of tea. He said she was a good egg.

We left him then and went back to the kitchen where we had cups of tea and soda scones. At the large table, Rosamund was sewing, Grace was learning French verbs and Genista's mother was just sitting, her elbows on the table and her face in her hands. Marigold and Bill Bryden were washing up, laughing a lot and splashing water at each other.

'Stop it, you two,' Rosamund said. 'My blouse is getting soaked. Why don't you grow up?'

I felt sorry for their father, sitting alone with his music and his haddock.

'Doesn't your father like being in the kitchen with the family?' I asked Genista later when we were upstairs in her bedroom. It was already eight o'clock and my father was coming to fetch me at half past.

'He and mother fall out about Maud Illingsworth,' she said. 'She was his model for years and years and he still likes her to visit. Anyway she'll be going back to London soon, so they'll make it up.'

'Was that Maud Illingsworth in his paintings?' I asked in a rush of surprise.

'Yes. Of course that was centuries ago. Her breasts are like tea plates now, Mother says. But he still likes to draw her, heaven knows why. She plays the oboe you know. Would you like to hear her?'

I wasn't sure I would, but all the same I nodded my head.

We went along to one of the rooms at the back of the house and as soon as Genista tapped on the door, it flew open and Maud Illingsworth practically fell out on us. She was dressed in a sort of long robe; pale pink.

'This is my friend, Elizabeth. She would like to hear you play the oboe.'

'Please come in. I'm afraid it's very cold. There doesn't seem to be any heating up here.' Her face was thin and still blue, but not ugly, not exactly. She looked as though she might be a distant relative of the woman in the paintings.

She fetched her oboe and after blowing into it and complaining that it was suffering from the cold, she started playing some music which was very sad and beautiful. I hadn't expected to like it, but I liked it a lot. It was a bit like a last bird at the end of the day.

Then she started on another piece which was even sadder than the first. It was a bit like winter and the cold, a bit like a woman thinking of the time she was young and happy, a bit like saying good-bye. I could hardly get my breath, that's how sad it was.

After a while Genista's mother came upstairs to listen. She stood by the half-open door and when she saw that I was crying, she cried too, and when the music had come to an end and the room was quiet again, she blew her nose and said, 'Please come down and have some supper, Maud. I've got a nice piece of haddock waiting for you.' There was another silence and then they patted each other on the shoulder and when Maud Illingsworth had put her oboe back into its black case, they went downstairs together.

One other thing happened before my father came for me.

Genista and I were down in the hall waiting for him when suddenly we heard a terrible rumpus upstairs, a lot of shouting and banging of doors and more shouting. 'Saints alive,' Genista said. And then Bill Bryden appeared and stamped down the stairs looking very sorry for himself and Marigold came rushing past him, flinging open the front door. 'Don't ever come back here,' she was shouting. 'I never, ever want to see you again.'

He didn't try to argue with her but just walked out into the pitch-black night.

I've never forgotten how miserable he looked or how black it was outside. Outside paradise.

Happy as Saturday Night

My Mum wakes me up at half nine on a Saturday because I has to go shopping for her. But I don't mind too much. As Janice says, you has to take the rough with the smooth, and the rest of Saturday is real smooth.

We lives on St Beuno's, a tough part of Cardiff about four miles from the centre. The food shops up here are terrible expensive. They says it's because they're always being vandalized and that, but if you asks me it's because they knows that mothers with lots of kids and no car will go to them whatever wicked prices they charge. Anyway I goes to Kwiksave and the market behind Tesco's for my Mum. She gives me twenty quid and a bit extra for a taxi home and I get her some great bargains. I finishes up with six or seven plastic bags which is why I need the taxi back. She's got three little ones and a new bloke and that's okay by me. She don't interfere with me and I don't interfere with her, and like I say, I don't begrudge the time I spends getting her shopping in.

I've got these good mates, see, and we has a great time on a Saturday. We works hard in the bleeding factory all week and it's all for Saturday night. Afternoons we might go to Goldees or Top Girl and try on some clothes and we like things that are sexy, real sexy I mean, we're not afraid of flaunting ourselves because we always sticks together, so we're always safe. My Mum tells me to get things from her club, but it's much cheaper where we goes and anyway by the time the catalogue stuff comes it's already past it. Last week I got a tight black satin dress and it looked like it had been painted on me with shiny gloss paint. That's the sort of thing we likes. And long glittery ear-rings and thick glittery eye shadow and pillar-box red lipstick, sticky as hot jam, that's the sort of thing we goes for.

We always sticks together. As soon as we've had our tea, we'll all be at Kim's house or Sian's – where there's no kids to bother us – and we has steaming hot bubble baths and then we does each other's hair, either blow-dry or tongs, with masses of volumizer and mousse. We goes in for Harlequin colour rinses too. I'm Titian Red this week and Kim's Raven Wing, and the others, shades of blonde; Ash, Strawberry and Honey. And we borrows each other's perfume sprays so we smells terrific, the lads at the bus stop can smell us coming before they sees us.

We aims for the half-nine which gets us into town around ten and first off we goes to the Prince of Wales for a couple of vodkas which really gets us in the mood. There's five of us altogether. Four of us was at school together, that's Ellie, Kim, Sian and me, we've been mates forever, and Janice is Ellie's big sister but she's ever so nice. She's twenty-one or two, but she acts like seventeen, she's really one of us now. She started coming out with us to keep an eye on Ellie because she's the youngest of us and a real dare-devil, and their mother ended up in one of them rest hospitals – you know – so Janice looks out for Ellie, but not in a bossy way.

Janice has got a husband and a kiddie, but her bloke don't mind her coming out clubbing with us on a Saturday night, he says it keeps her young and frisky. And besides he goes out with the lads on a Friday night and darts on a Tuesday, so fair's fair, I say, though my Mum thinks he's some sort of super guy, some sort of a new man, she says, too good to be true. His name's Charlie. I don't know him very well. Ellie says he's great, but whenever she says it, Kim and Sian say, 'Well, he fancies you, doesn't he, oh yes, two for the price of one.' But I don't listen because it's not the sort of thing I likes to think about because of Janice. The baby's about a year old and he's called Jake.

Anyway, this one Saturday, Charlie goes out shopping with Janice and buys her a new dress. We're all ever so pleased because she can't spend so much on clothes as us single girls because of the rent and that. It's a brilliant dress too, gooseberry green crushed velvet and so tight you can see her belly button as well as her nipples and the cleft in her bum, and she's got a nice tan from spending her lunch-times in the park with Jake – he goes to Happy Times Crèche but she has him out every lunch-time – and Kim got her some tattoo stickers for her shoulders, two bluebirds on one and a pink heart on the other, she looked terrific. We was all pretty lush that Saturday, but she was dead lush, I mean it.

Well, I suppose it's about half past eleven when we goes sauntering down to Roxanne's in Dominion Street, the vodka we'd had making us very happy, giggling at everything and whistling at these rugby fellas, big and stupid as tanks, still standing outside the rugby pubs with their pints.

The bouncers outside Roxanne's are ever so friendly. 'Go home, girls, and put some decent clothes on your backs,' they says when they sees us, but all in fun. After ten minutes or so in the Ladies, putting on fresh lipstick and hairspray and that, we goes in and starts dancing, the five of us together. Then this bloke comes up to Ellie and manages to lure her away, but he's from up our way and anyway we knows Janice will be keeping an eye on her.

About one, one thirty, there's this terrific dazzle of lights and an announcement: 'Hold on to your knickers, ladies, our stripper has arrived. And it's South Wales's answer to the Chippendales, it's our very own Mark Emmanuel from Abercrave.' There's some half-hearted clapping from the girls and some groaning from the fellas and then this very loud Fifties music and here he is, Mark Emmanuel himself, very cool, singing 'Blue Suede Shoes' and taking off his white jacket and his tie as though he's God's own gift.

And I suppose he has got something too, because I starts thinking about sex, how I'm always turned on by words like fuck and shag, but how I don't want to do anything about it just yet because I remember how everyone used to say I'd love it in Big School, but I really missed being in the Infants where all we done was play around with coloured paper and paste and that, and in Big School you had to start learning your letters and doing sums and teachers stopped being nice to you.

Well, I'm half-way through school by now, fourth year at Maesderw Road Comprehensive, when I suddenly sees that Mark Emmanuel is down to his G-string and all the girls but me shouting

'Off, off, off,' and all of a sudden he comes right over to where we're standing and he's asking Ellie to go out the front with him, what for I don't quite know, but I suppose I can guess.

Ellie's got such a baby face and that's what seems to turn fellas on more than anything. She's seventeen, like me and Kim and Sian, but she looks like a dressed-up twelve year old, the way she stands with her feet turned out, her eyes big and glistening and her top lip not quite covering her teeth. Kim says she looks just like the girls laying back on fur rugs in her Dad's porno magazines, but I swear she can't help it, it's just natural to her, that half timid, half come-on way of looking.

And then everyone's urging Ellie to go out the front where there's this circle of lights focusing on Mark Emmanuel, and at last, looking back rather proudly at us, she goes off with him and he tries to get her to pull his G-string off. Anyway, she hangs back and he thinks she's playing it clever to keep the tension up, but Janice isn't fooled and she goes out the front to get her away. And then Mark Emmanuel switches his attention to Janice, but she's not having any, she slaps his hand away, only not to hurt, and she pulls Ellie back to where we're standing, and he finishes his act on his own, shows us his thing, and we all squeal politely – like we're supposed to – and then he puts on one of these black silk kimonos and sings more smoochy songs and that's the end of that.

Only it's not, because Ellie wants to see him after. She says he told her to go round to his dressing room and she's mad keen to go, but Janice says she can't unless we all goes with her and she has to be satisfied with that.

He seems a bit surprised to see all five of us, but he takes it in good part and gives us a drink each in a paper cup – it tastes a bit dusty – and asks did we like his act and we all says yes, but it's not Ellie he's trying to make it with now, but Janice, staring into her eyes and begging for it.

'We must go,' she says, very firm, 'or we won't manage to get a taxi. It was nice meeting you, Mark.'

He gives us all a kiss as we leave, but at the last minute he makes a grab at Janice who's last out the door, and pulls her back. We can hear a scuffle and we don't know whether to go back in or not, but in no time at all she's out again, but looking wild, her eyes gushing over with tears and her gorgeous new dress all torn up the back.

'Just look at you,' Ellie says, as though it was Janice wanting to go round not her. 'Your new dress is ruined and serves you right.'

It's okay,' Kim says. 'It's only the seam and my Mum will run that up for you on her Singer.'

'It's not okay,' Janice says, and now she's crying real hard. And Ellie marches off with the other two following her, so after a bit I goes with Janice to find the manager and we tells him she caught her dress on a nail and we don't like to go out like that. And he says not to worry, and he finds her a long white mac someone's left behind and then we has to go because by now everyone's gone, even the bouncers, and the manager wants to lock up.

There's no sign of the others when we gets out and we haven't got the money for a taxi because we always chips in one fifty each and no one would take Janice and me to St Beuno's for three pounds, which is all we've got left. (To tell you the truth the taxi drivers aren't any too happy taking all five of us, but we tells them we're all under eight stone, so it's only like taking two and a half big blokes and then they're generally okay.)

Anyway, there's nothing for it but to walk so we starts straight away. I've never liked bloody walking. Even in the country, even in daylight, even with some half-decent shoes on, it's dead boring if you ask me, but this is a nightmare, grey streets, a mean wind from the river and both of us miserable, me because the others couldn't be bothered to wait for us and Janice because of her torn dress and being late home. We hardly says a word to each other the whole way.

By the time we gets to my house I'm dying for my bed, but I haven't got the heart to let Janice walk the last half mile on her own. 'Look, I'll come with you,' I tells her. 'You're a good pal,' she says. 'You can sleep on the sofa and Charlie'll run you home in the van tomorrow.' 'Okay,' I says.

Their flat is four floors up and the smell in the passage makes you want to throw up, but I don't say anything, just drags myself up the endless stairs.

When we gets to the hallway we can hear the baby grizzling and Janice says, 'Oh hell, I bet Charlie hasn't fed him. I'll have to do it. Will you have a cup of tea?'

I offers to make it and she says to excuse the mess because she didn't have time to wash up the tea things and she doesn't clean through till the Sunday. So she fetches the baby and gives him his bottle while I makes us cups of tea and hands one to her.

After his feed, Jake wakes up good and proper and wants to play, but neither of us has the energy so he plays with the beer cans Charlie's left around the floor and we just sits and watches him like two old biddies.

After about five minutes building up the cans and knocking them down again, Jake gets sleepy and Janice pops him back in his cot which is in the corner of the lounge and then she gets a tee-shirt for me to sleep in and a blanket and tucks me up on the sofa. 'I hope Ellie's okay,' she says to me last thing. 'Of course she is,' I tells her.

I'm drifting off to sleep when I hears this commotion from somewhere. At first I think it's someone in the next flat, but then I recognizes Janice's voice and she's crying and saying, 'I couldn't help it. It wasn't my fault. I couldn't help it,' and Charlie's shouting, calling her a slag and calling Ellie a slag and even calling her mother a slag. And then there's another sort of noise and Janice shouting, 'No. Please. No, no, no.' And I pulls the blanket right over my head because I knows exactly what's going on but I'm too frightened to get up and help her. I just have to lay there and listen to it, the thud, thud, thud, thud, thud, until it suddenly stops.

And then I can't get to sleep again. Suddenly I hates life. Sunday afternoon when I has to go and see my miserable old Gran and then getting up at seven on Monday and all the week and working at the sausage factory with all the smells you can't get used to. It all seems too much to bear.

I'm on the point of having a good howl when I feels

Janice's hand on my shoulder. 'Can I squeeze in with you?' she says. And I moves right up against the wall and puts my arm around her, and after a while she stops crying and we gets nice and warm.

'It'll be okay next Saturday, won't it?' Janice says, still sniffing a bit.

'Course it will,' I tells her. 'Next Saturday's going to be bloody brilliant.'

And Perhaps More

The small chapel was only half full, the singing uncertain. Suddenly a watery sun slanted in through the arched window and lit up the young minister's face so that for a moment or two he looked almost saintly, his closely-barbered fair hair and his skin glowing. The singing grew more confident. There was an attempt at harmony.

Glyn felt uncomfortable that the young chap - he couldn't have been more than twenty-three or four - referred to his newly-dead mother as Hester; she was Mrs Richards to everyone outside the family and wouldn't have approved his over-familiarity. Of course, the young minister didn't know her, she hadn't been to chapel for the last couple of years.

'Have you lost your Faith?' Glyn had once asked her. 'Oh no, I don't think so, love. It's just that I can't get in to my chapel shoes, that's all, and it doesn't seem worth buying any more. In my old wellingtons all day and your father's slippers about the house, my feet have got swollen, that's all.'

Glyn suddenly remembered a scene from Romeo and Juliet which he'd done for O-level, years ago. A bit far-fetched to his way of thinking, all that killing each other's cousins and dying for love. But Mr Montague had been real enough at that party at the beginning of the play, 'Now come on and dance,' he'd said, 'at least all of you ladies that haven't got corns.' He'd liked that.

Shakespeare certainly knew a bit about elderly people's feet.

He tried to keep his mind on the minister's words, but they didn't seem to have much connection with his mother. Had his mother ever *Lived in the Lord* as he seemed to be suggesting? Glyn couldn't see it like that. To his way of thinking, his mother was altogether more earth-bound; had worked hard all her life - and died disappointed. And it was his fault. He was forty years old with no wife and no child. So that the farm was blighted, fated to fail.

As far as he was aware, his mother knew nothing of the Romeo and Juliet variety of love, but she was always stressing that love, family love, was essential on a farm to make all the hard work worthwhile. 'Get yourself a nice sweetheart,' she'd beg Glyn over and over. 'And if at first you don't succeed, try, try again.'

When he was young, Glyn had put his back into the quest. But the farm was on an unclassified mountain road, eleven miles from the nearest small town, three from the nearest village and by that time girls had decent jobs in Building Societies and Estate Agents and didn't want to be farmers' wives. Or at least no-one wanted to be his wife. Even twenty years ago he was overweight and nothing of a talker. He'd persevered though, for several years, being everyone's best friend at the Young Farmers' weekly meetings, having a good laugh with all the girls, driving them here and there, buying them drinks, but never able to establish a special relationship with one of them.

'I'm giving up,' he'd announced just after Christmas one year. 'There's only so much fun a person can be doing with.'

'Don't give up,' his mother had begged. 'Please don't give

up.'

He looked across at his mother's sister, his Auntie Phyllis, and her son, Hywel. Hywel was a prosperous dentist with a good practice in Newtown, a pretty wife called Jennifer and two children; a boy and a girl of course, everything falling snap into place. A good-natured chap, though, he had to admit. 'Why don't you get married, man?' he'd ask afterwards, when they were back in the lonely, isolated farmhouse. 'It's not as bad as everyone makes out and there's plenty of compensations.' 'Oh, I'm looking around,' Glyn would reply, that false, comradely note in his voice. What if he answered, 'Because no-one will bloody have me, Hywel, that's why. And why should they? I'm not handsome and self-assured like you, but flabby and tongue-tied. If I was a woman, I'd run a mile sooner than have anything to do with a soft-centered bloke like me.'

He suddenly remembered that it was through Hywel that he'd first met Carol-Ann; the only woman who had really touched his heart. He'd only spoken to her a few times in all, but he'd felt close to her, perhaps because he'd dreamed of someone like her for so long. She had a lovely calm smile and eyes clear as water and she was not too thin nor too fat. Hywel had introduced her to his mother when both women had happened to be in hospital at the same time, both recovering from minor operations. 'Carol-Ann used to be my receptionist, Auntie,' he'd said, whispering afterwards, 'nice, hard-working girl. One of the best.'

His mother had found Carol-Ann good company, interested in the same television programmes, the same magazines, the same knitting patterns, and prepared to listen to all her anxieties about the sheep and the new lambs. Before she'd left, she'd invited her up to the farm for Sunday dinner, a meal usually restricted to close relatives.

'I've found you a girl-friend,' she'd announced, when Glyn had come to fetch her home. 'Well, I had to, didn't I, because you don't seem to be getting anywhere on your own. She's a lovely girl, too, quiet, but hard-working and dependable according to your cousin, Hywel. She was once his receptionist, it seems, and she's very interested to meet you.'

Glyn sighed as he remembered the day Carol-Ann had come up to the farm. He'd had such hopes - it was about fifteen years ago, before he'd begun to feel so worthless. His mother had talked of her for over a week, but as soon as she arrived, she turned against her: she'd brought her three-year old son with her and had confessed to being an unmarried mother. Only it wasn't as much of a confession as an assertion. 'This is my little lad, Mrs Richards. No, I'm not married. It didn't work out.' She'd sounded perfectly self-assured, but Glyn had noticed that her hands were tightly clenched together.

Glyn himself hadn't held it against her, he thought she was very brave, managing so well on her own and seeming immensely proud of little Mark. He had got on splendidly with the little lad, but had failed to make any headway with Carol-Ann. If only he'd been able to swing her up in his arms, as he did Mark, and take her out to see the lambs, they might have got somewhere, but with her he could only sweat and stammer and pull at his collar. His mother hadn't invited her back either, but kept saying they'd had a lucky escape. Glyn had thought about her for months, even years.

After that disappointment, he'd been quiet and depressed, again refusing to go out.

'How can you meet anyone stuck in the house every Saturday night?' his mother would ask. 'You know we've got money. Over a hundred thousand safe in the bank since we sold that strip of land for bungalows, and doing all right besides. Your wife would have her own car and every modern convenience, calor gas central heating, a bathroom and separate toilet. When I married your father we didn't even have an inside tap. Why don't you put a little advert in the Gazette? Everyone seems to be doing it these days.'

After a while he'd relented. 'Farmer with thriving farm w.l.t.m. middle-aged woman for pleasant evenings out and perhaps more.'

Maureen, raven-haired and big-chested, had been the only one to reply. She'd let him give her expensive Friday evening dinners for several weeks, permitting him to kiss her briefly as they parted, but refusing all his invitations to visit the farm. Then, when he'd offered to run her home one snowy evening, she'd confessed that she was married and that perhaps they shouldn't meet again.

The worst of it was that he'd grown very fond of her, admiring the way she so indomitably tackled twelve pieces of cutlery and gargantuan meals, while talking away on genteel subjects like the *Antiques Road Show* and growing delphiniums. Most men were scathing of women, but he really liked them; their strange affectations, their absurdly impractical shoes, the haughty faces they made at themselves in mirrors, their smooth skin, the smell of their make-up and perfume; and some darker smell too, like ferns on a river bank.

He joined a dating agency, but no woman had lasted the course, in fact few had accepted a second date. His mother always told him how smart he looked in his navy-blue suit and maroon tie, but though he did his best, taking the women to restaurants, concerts and films, treating them with care and deference, he failed to capture their interest. He remembered all of them with affection; Rhian was much too young for him, but he'd driven her all the way to Liverpool to some rock concert she'd set her heart on, managing to get her a ticket and waiting outside to drive her back. He remembered with pleasure how she'd thanked him so nicely and slept on his shoulder all the way home. Maxine was a hairdresser, not at all pretty, but she laughed a lot and he loved the way her lips didn't quite meet over her teeth. Lowri squinted when she was nervous, but she was tall and slender like a thoroughbred pony. She'd agreed to meet him for the second time, but had written a polite letter telling him that a previous boy-friend had contacted her again. She said she'd enjoyed meeting him and hoped he wouldn't think badly of her. He still had the letter.

After a year with the agency, a year of these pleasant but very short-lived relationships, he'd given up and started thinking of himself as the eternal bachelor. But his mother hadn't forgiven him. 'Think of the farm,' she'd say, over and over again. 'Who's going to run the farm when you've gone?'

'I'm sorry,' a voice inside him wept as the coffin was

lowered into the ground. 'I'm sorry. I was a failure. I let you down.'

His Auntie Phyllis noticed his tears and took his arm. She had married an auctioneer and was the lady president of the Rotary Club. She was dressed totally in black, a little hat like a black nest perched on her head. Glyn was aware that she hadn't done enough for his mother during her long, last illness, but could see that she felt guilty about it and was trying to atone. Later on she would be a Tower of Strength. She would fling open windows. She would produce mountains of sandwiches for the neighbours. She would pack away his mother's clothes to give to charity. She would make lists. He squeezed her hand.

There weren't as many people back in the house as he'd feared. He made up the fire, talked football to the young minister, nodded and smiled at everyone who sympathised with him, and carried round cups of tea. Somehow the time passed and the neighbours left.

Hywel's wife, Jennifer, was the next who wanted to leave. 'No, I'm bloody staying,' Hywel said. 'Taking Glyn out for a drink later on. Just stop moaning for once.'

'Oh please, sweetie,' she kept saying, pulling at her husband's arm and turning large moist eyes at him. 'Oh, please. You know we've got to get the kiddies back from my parents and put them to bed before we can leave them with the baby-sitter. Oh sweetie, you said ....'

Glyn could see Hywel becoming more and more exasperated, until at last he'd thrown her arm back at her and broken away. 'Come out for a breath of air, man,' he urged Glyn who was hovering about uneasily. 'Leave the washing-up to the women.'

'She wants to go to some blessed dinner-party tonight,' he said when they were outside. 'I don't feel like socialising, but she won't take no for an answer.'

Glyn tried to change the subject. 'I was sorry not to see Jason and Melissa.'

'She wouldn't let them come, man. It would have done them good. I want them to have a sense of family and a sense of place. God, they're eleven and nine now, not babies. They can't be protected from everything for ever.' He turned fiercely towards his cousin. 'You don't know how lucky you are, man.'

'Not to have a wife?' Glyn asked, thinking the question might bring Hywel to his senses.

'Better not have a wife than the wrong one,' Hywel replied, as bitterly as before.

'Now, steady on, Hywel. You don't mean that. Don't let a little tiff get you down. Go to the bloody dinner-party tonight. It'll do you good. What's the use of staying in to brood? Think yourself lucky. Jennifer is a very good-looking young woman and anyone can see how fond she is of you.'

'Fond of what I can give her,' Hywel muttered, but with less anger than before. 'Anyway, it's you we should be talking about not me. How the hell are you going to manage up here on your own? I'm worried about you, man.'

'I'll be all right, I suppose. After all, mother hasn't been able to do much for the last couple of years, has she?'

'But she was always good company, Auntie Hester. She

was genuine, a real person. Know what I mean? Not always trying to be somebody else, somebody different, somebody grand.' He kicked at a stone. 'Not like all the bloody women I know,' he said, suddenly as savage as before.

They came to a five-bar gate and leaned over it. 'You never tried to make a go of it with Carol-Ann?' Hywel asked. 'Auntie Hester seemed all for it.'

'No, she wasn't. Not once she realised about the boy. Not once she realised she was an unmarried mother.'

'What about you, though?'

'Oh, I thought she was lovely, but what chance did I have. What chance would I have with anyone, let alone someone my mother disapproved of. No guts, Hywel, that's my trouble. And no way with women either.'

'She liked you, she told me that much, thought you were very kind.'

'Yes, very kind. That's what all women think about me. I saw her again last summer, but she didn't see me. Or at least, pretended not to.'

'She's lost her looks,' Hywel said, kicking another stone.

'I don't know about that. She's put on a bit of weight, but I thought it suited her. Such a smile she had. Did a man good to see it.'

'Her son, Mark, do you remember him?'

'Great little chap, I thought. Duw, I can still remember how he charged after those lambs I had.'

'He's in trouble, man. A teenager now. Bit of a tearaway.

Been in one of these remand centres for six months. She's worried sick about him, about what he'll do when he gets out. Nothing for him in Newtown, nothing but hanging around with the wrong crowd.' There was a short silence during which both men looked about them and then at each other. 'Look here Glyn, I was wondering whether you could see your way to giving him some sort of job up here with you. Give him some measure of independence that would, some self-assurance.'

Glyn felt an icy wind clearing his head. 'Your lad, is he?' he asked gently.

A moment's pause, both men staring hard at the mountains, at the rain clouds gathering.

'Aye. My lad. Should have married her, of course, but I was engaged to Jennifer by that time and her father taking me into the practice. And Carol-Ann not the sort to fight. Oh Glyn, I've been a right sod all my life.'

'There's plenty worse,' Glyn said. He meant it, too. He knew Hywel was suffering. There was something decent about him at the core.

'I envy you, Glyn. You've got nothing to reproach yourself for.'

'Oh, I have. I let my mother down. Gave up too soon. Was too easily cast down. All she asked was for me to get married and have children. All she wanted was children to inherit this terrible, soul-breaking place.'

They stood together watching the clouds shifting, the colours of the distant mountains change from slate-blue to charcoal.

'You love the place,' Hywel said.

'Do I? I don't know. Love or hate, it's all the same at six in the morning.' Glyn suddenly straightened up. 'Anyway, I'll be pleased to have the lad if he can bear to come here. I'll do my best for him. He's my blood, after all.'

'You're a saint, man. I said to Carol-Ann the other day, "If anyone is willing to give him a helping hand, that'll be my cousin, Glyn."'

'I'll do my best, that's all I've said. A decent wage. And I'll get him a little car too, so he can go to town in the evenings. I won't keep him a prisoner, I can promise you that, and I won't work him too hard, either. But he may have different ideas of what he wants to do and I won't think any the worse of him for that.'

The two men stood looking hard at each other for a moment or two. 'And now we'll go back,' Glyn continued. 'And you must make it up with Jennifer and go to that dinner-party.'

They turned and walked slowly towards the farmhouse. 'Carol-Ann is married by this time, I suppose?' Glyn asked, with some attempt at lightness.

'Well, she is....she is....with someone,' Hywel said, refusing to meet his eyes.

'Yes, I thought as much. A lovely woman.'

Hywel turned towards him. 'Don't envy me, Glyn,' he said in a half-strangled voice. 'You're a free man and a good un.'

A lapwing circled above them, its harsh, desolate cry seeming to mock both of them.